GOLD OF THE BAR 10

Gene Adams and his riders of the Bar 10 had brought in a herd of steers and been paid. Deciding to visit friends, Adams, Tomahawk, Johnny Puma and Red Hawke retrace an old trail on their way back to Texas. But an outlaw gang trails them, interested in the gold in Adams' saddlebags. And ahead of them two killers have kidnapped Johnny's sweetheart, Nancy . . . Can these legendary riders survive the dangers looming on all sides?

BOYD CASSIDY

GOLD OF THE BAR 10

Complete and Unabridged

LINFORD
Leicester

First published in Great Britain in 2005 by
Robert Hale Limited
London

Cassidy, Boyd
    Gold of the bar 10.—Large print ed.—
Linford western library
1. Western stories
2. Large type books
I. Title
823.9'14 [F]

ISBN 1–84617–472–4

Published by
F. A. Thorpe (Publishing)
Anstey, Leicestershire

Set by Words & Graphics Ltd.
Anstey, Leicestershire
Printed and bound in Great Britain by
T. J. International Ltd., Padstow, Cornwall

This book is printed on acid-free paper

*Dedicated with heartfelt thanks to
Karla Buhlman and
Kim Mansfield.*

Prologue

There have been many legends in the history of what we now refer to as the Wild West. Some legends were memorable events whilst others concerned individuals who carved their names in the granite of our collective worship. Some were good and some were bad. Yet of all the heroes who lived during those dangerous times, one name stands out as a beacon to all.

A name that has become recognized as that of one of the West's greatest sons. A Texan who, like those who defended the Alamo so long before, refused to even consider running away from trouble. His kind never retreated.

Like ancient oaks, they stood firm.

He was a man who never cheated, never lied and never drew his famed golden Colts on anyone who had not tried to kill him first. A man who never started a fight and yet he always finished them.

Gene Lon Adams was a unique character who became known and feared in his own long lifetime. A man whose sheer grit earned him the respect of all who ever encountered his tanned features and snow-white hair.

Adams was a man who, it seemed, had never been young as most of us are once young. A man who appeared never to grow old, as is our ultimate fate.

Gene Adams was that rarest of creatures: a man who never seemed to change at all. Or if he did, nobody seemed to notice. He was an enigma. A man who always remained exactly the same.

Tall, tanned and tough.

Yet always fair.

It was the way he had lived his life.

His every action ruled by an unwritten code.

But it is not just Gene Adams himself who has gone down in history. His beloved million-acre cattle ranch in the heart of Texas has also become the place of legend. Its fame has grown into almost mythical proportions. Today few can even agree exactly where the Bar 10 ranch was situated. Like its courageous owner, the ranch itself has become the stuff of legend.

As with ancient Camelot every red-blooded Texan secretly believes that the location of the Bar 10 is somehow near them. If not, it should be.

Legendary exploits not only of Gene Adams but of his closest friends, Tomahawk and Johnny Puma, as well as all the other famed riders of the Bar 10, grow with every telling.

Stories that are always of good pitted against evil, like the characters themselves, never die.

Adams and his two most loyal companions, Johnny Puma and Tomahawk, had set out from McCoy with the proceeds of their latest cattle drive. After putting the rest of the Bar 10 cowboys and their mounts on a train, the three riders headed out to rediscover old trails and even older friends.

But they would soon realize that they were not alone on their journey back to the Bar 10.

Soon they found danger stalking their every move.

Even in the Wild West, some had no respect for legends.

1

The wide streets of cattle town McCoy were filled to overflowing with the strange array of people that always accumulated whenever a large herd of prime beef on the hoof was driven up from Texas for auction. They came from everywhere as if drawn like moths to a light. So many people filled the streets, either buying or selling, that they even sprawled out on to the dusty roads and competed with the normal traffic of riders and vehicles. Auction day was always something special. McCoy came to life when the stock-pens that lined the railtracks were filled with well-fattened steers. Thousands of extra people moved in every direction like ants on a termite hill. So many people had flocked into the railhead town that the half-dozen riders who rode silently in single file down the main street went totally unnoticed.

There was an old saying that the best place to hide was in a crowd. The six horsemen, draped in their long dust-coats, knew that it was true. For when your image is on countless wanted posters and you are wanted dead or alive, it is always wiser to frequent large towns or cities, rather than small ones.

In a small settlement where the sheriff knows every face by name, any stranger is immediately under suspicion. Far better to ride into places where there are simply too many faces for the law to check.

The six horsemen were here for a purpose. It had nothing to do with robbing any of the banks which had sprouted up over the previous decade. Nor did it have anything to do with holding up any of the trains which continuously moved in and out of the big town. These outlaws had an easier target in their sights. One that would reap them rich rewards and, if executed properly, would go unnoticed long enough for them to reach the safety of neutral territories.

The deadly lead rider, Samson Stone, had once been an honest man. Yet that had been long ago, before his taste for expensive things overruled his strict Methodist upbringing.

Like so many greedy people before him, Stone had wanted things he knew no honest man of his limited abilities could ever acquire. Driven by an insane jealousy of all those who had more than he himself had, the then youngster had vowed to take what he wanted by any means available. It had not taken him long to realize that the meagre investment in a second-hand Smith & Wesson .44 would reap profits and benefits beyond most people's wildest imaginings.

For someone who had been so strictly raised to be God-fearing like all of his kind, he took to killing easily.

Far too easily.

The bullets had not been in the gun's chambers for more than ten hours before the killing had started. Stone had never really given his deadly actions a second thought. Never felt guilty for his slayings. In many ways he had convinced himself that what he was doing was not truly evil at all. For a man who never travelled without a copy of the Bible on his person, it had been easy for him to consider himself working for a higher being.

Not a deadly outlaw at all, but an avenging angel. Sent to destroy all that is evil and corrupt in the land. It was an insanity that had afflicted many others over the years.

Yet for the most part, his victims were innocents. Their only crime was to have something that the outlaw wanted. Few if any had ever been able to defend themselves against the ferocity of Stone's lethal guns.

Samson Stone led his five followers into McCoy the same way as he had done in countless other towns over the years. It had become a well-practised exercise designed by Stone himself and honed to perfection. No rider ever rode closer than twenty feet from the one before him. They would allow their mounts to wander around buckboards, wagons and stagecoaches so as not to draw attention to themselves.

The sextet of riders had done exactly the same thing more times than any of them could recall. They entered a town and knew that if they did not draw attention to themselves, they could achieve exactly what they wanted.

Few had ever wasted more than a fleeting glance upon any of them. Yet these six horsemen were worthy of anyone's studied attention. Scrutinizing the faces for a few moments might have made the more alert of the town's lawmen realize that they had visitors with high price-tags on their heads riding into McCoy.

The long dust-coats were not uncommon on riders who used the dry dusty trails between the remote settlements which were scattered throughout the West. But for Stone and his five men they served not only to keep the trail grime off their clothes, they also hid the array of weaponry that the men sported.

Even the slowest of onlookers might have become a little suspicious of men who were so well-heeled with guns and ammunition belts.

Dust-coats could cover a lot of sins.

Since he had first used a gun, Stone had managed to kill more than sixty men, women and sometimes children, during his unholy existence. His riders were no less brutal than himself, although only he tended to misquote his Bible in order to justify his actions.

They simply killed.

Booker Talbot was the most dangerous of all the men who rode with Stone. He had served time and lost all respect for anything remotely to do with the law. He had vowed that he would rather die than ever go back to prison. Yet his fears about ever serving time again were ill-founded. If the law ever did catch up with Booker again, the Wanted poster on his head would ensure he would be hanged from the nearest tree.

Carson Farmer and Zon Mooney had ridden together long before they encountered Stone. Yet it had been Stone that had turned them from petty opportunistic thieves into the hardened killers they now were.

They owed him a lot.

Leroy Chard had been enlisted by Samson Stone only a few years earlier when he needed an expert marksman to pick off an entire posse before they had even managed to ride out of the boundaries of their town. Chard had few equals with a rifle.

The rider who brought up the rear was Poke Green. He was around the same age as Stone, and yet looked far older. His long white hair hung from under the brim of his broad-brimmed Stetson and bounced on his shoulder. He was probably the most important of Stone's five followers. He watched his fellow outlaws ahead of him, and also surveyed the countless faces of the

11

townspeople in case any of the gang were recognized. For trouble often reared its head and it was Green's job to stop it as quickly and silently as possible.

Samson Stone knew that although he and all his men were wanted dead or alive for the accumulated sum of $5,000, their true value would have been ten times that if they had been linked to all their brutal crimes.

Stone had a knack of managing to strike and ride long before anyone knew what had occurred. Crimes in remote places hardly ever got recorded. That was the way the Bible-puncher liked it. He liked to swoop down on his prey in places where few ever ventured.

Even before he had drawn rein Stone knew roughly what he was going to do. He had only to find out who his victims would be, then calculate where he would set his trap.

News of the auction had spread far and wide long before Adams had led his herd into McCoy. Samson Stone already had the name of his chosen target before he dismounted outside the auction house near the railtracks. All the outlaw had to do now was find out what the man looked like and then try and learn more about his route back to Texas.

'If it ain't Gene Adams. Howdy, Gene,' the auctioneer bellowed as he strode past Stone and up to the tall rancher. He shook the gloved hand firmly. 'I got two darn big bags of fifty-dollar gold coins in my safe waiting for you. C'mon.'

'That's mighty fine, Cecil.' Gene Adams smiled. 'I'm obliged.'

Samson Stone looped his reins around the hitching pole and tied a firm knot. He watched the Bar 10 man trail the auctioneer up the weathered steps and enter the red-painted building. He looked at his five men who were scattered around the large area.

It had begun.

2

Gene Adams had no idea that since he had left the auctioneer's office near the rail tracks, his every move had been watched by six pairs of eyes. The rancher dismounted his tall chestnut mare and carefully untied the hefty saddle-bags from behind the high cantle. Before he had turned and stepped up on to the boardwalk outside the saloon, all twenty of his Bar 10 cowboys had surrounded him.

'Reckon I ought to pay you boys your bonus money.' Adams smiled as Tomahawk moved close to the man who held the heavy weight in his left hand.

There was a collective sound of agreement.

Adams walked up the steps and entered the busy saloon, flanked by his loyal cowboys.

'Make way for the Bar 10!' Adams

shouted out above the sound of a tinny piano and numerous noisy saloon patrons.

The crowd parted like the Red Sea when it saw Moses. Adams marched like a general leading his troops to his usual group of tables at the far corner of the drinking-hole.

'How many bottles of whiskey does the Bar 10 want?' a bartender called out across the saloon.

Adams dropped the bags on top of a green-baize card-table and aimed a gloved finger at the bartender.

'Beers all round, barkeep.'

'Ah, shucks,' Tomahawk grumbled as he found a chair and seated himself. 'We never gets to drink whiskey. How come?'

'Because we are heading home in a couple of hours,' Adams said, unbuckling one of the satchels. 'Whiskey makes a man ornery, you know that.'

'But it can add lead to ya pencil, boy.' Tomahawk sniffed.

'Ha!' Adams gave a belly laugh.

'What do you need lead in your pencil for, Tomahawk? You ain't got nobody to write to.'

Adams dished out the bonus gold coins to his men and then buckled the satchel again. He was enjoying himself for the first time in months. The worry of the cattle-drive was at long last behind him.

Adams had just finished his second glass of beer when a voice rang out from across the bar.

'See ya still riding high and wide, Adams!'

'Who said that?' Tomahawk asked.

'Easy, old-timer.' Adams said.

'Over yonder, Gene.' Johnny Puma pointed. 'Near the keno tables.'

The rancher placed the glass down and stood to see who it was who had called out to him. His eyes narrowed when he spotted a face he had not seen in over two decades.

'Is that you, Black Tom?' Adams asked, moving away from the card table and his men.

'Ya knows it is, ya cheatin' swine!' Black Tom Cotter snapped as he moved away from the keno-players. 'Bet ya thought I was dead, huh?'

'I have to admit it, Black Tom,' Adams said, squaring up to the well-built man. 'I sure hoped you was dead by now.'

Half the saloon laughed. The other half went deadly silent.

'I told ya I'd be back,' Cotter snarled.

'Yep. You sure did. Mind you, that was twenty years ago.'

Johnny moved to Adams's shoulder.

'He's got himself two low-hung Colts there, Gene. You want me to handle him?'

Adams did not take his eyes off Cotter.

'Sit down, Johnny. I know how to handle filth. No need for you to get your hands dirty.'

Cotter took two steps forward.

'Did ya just call me filth, Adams?'

Gene Adams inhaled and stood firm.

'I sure did, Black Tom. You were

always filth. Reckon I ain't never met a two-legged critter more filthy than you. And I've met me an awful lot of critters.'

The interior of the saloon fell quiet. So quiet that the ticking of the wall clock seemed to echo off the wooden walls.

Black Tom Cotter flexed his fingers and allowed both his hands to hover over his gun grips.

'Took me a while to get out of the pen. Then I had to come half-way across the country to find ya. Now I'm here and you is gonna die.'

The Bar 10 cowboys began to move.

Adams waved at them.

'Stay where you are, boys. This is between me and Black Tom.'

Cotter lowered his head. His eyes burned across the distance between them.

'Draw!'

Adams smiled. This time it was not the smile of an amused man but the warning smile of someone who had used his precious golden Colts to remain alive in a hostile land.

'I'll draw when you do!'

Cotter went for his guns. Adams did not draw but grabbed a hardback chair and threw it straight at the gunman. The chair hit Cotter in his face. He staggered as the rancher strode quickly up to him. Before Black Tom knew what was happening, Adams sent a clenched left fist into the man's belly as he drove a right cross hard on to the unshaven jaw.

Cotter fell on to his knees. Adams grabbed both Cotter's Colts out of their holsters and tossed them over the bar counter, then he dragged the stunned figure back up. He smashed his right fist into the middle of Cotter's face.

The largest of the saloon's windows shattered as Black Tom went crashing through it and landed heavily on to the boardwalk.

Adams pulled his gloves tight over his hands and turned to Rip Calloway and Happy Summers.

'Go rope that maverick and take him to the sheriff,' Adams ordered. 'Tell him to keep Black Tom locked up until we've left McCoy.' He returned to the table and sat down between Tomahawk and Johnny.

'What was that all about, Gene?' Tomahawk asked. 'Who is that *hombre*?'

'Don't you remember Black Tom?' Adams accepted a fresh glass of beer and swallowed half of it. 'He got darned upset with me about twenty years back.'

'What for?'

'I killed three of his brothers,' Adams muttered. 'He got a tad upset.'

'Ya killed three of his kinfolk? How come?'

'They was trying to bushwhack me,' Adams replied. 'They weren't no good at it though. Just like Black Tom ain't never been any good with those Colts of his.'

The rancher and his cowboys had no way of knowing that the six outlaws had been watching and listening to all that was going on in the saloon. One by one they drifted out of the swing-doors and into the sunshine.

They knew now that their job was going to be a lot harder than they had first imagined. But Samson Stone was not afraid.

Only sane men felt that emotion.

3

Times were hard for the vast million acre cattle ranch. Gene Lon Adams had been forced to make a third cattle-drive to the distant McCoy since the start of the year to sell an additional 1,000 head of his prime longhorn steers. Adams had made nearly ten dollars a head for the well-fattened stock, but there had been a time when he would have made twice that amount. Most ranchers would have reduced the number of cowboys on the payroll when times were tough, but not Gene Adams. To him, the men who rode for the Bar 10 brand were like the sons he had never been blessed with. However hard times got, you did not fire kin. It was as simple as that.

It had been a hard drive this time. The trail to McCoy at the height of summer was dry. In a normal season,

Adams would not even have contemplated it. Too little water and less than enough sweet grass had dogged the trail drive. Yet it was over and the legendary owner of the Bar 10 had $10,000 in gold coin filling his saddle-bags. With luck, it would be enough to last until the new year.

The sun was high and hot as it had been for the previous six weeks, ever since they had set out on the treacherous trek. The riders of the Bar 10 were headed toward the rail spur just south of the famed cattle town. Adams, atop his tall chestnut mare, was leading his twenty trail-weary cowboys to the place that he knew would provide them and their horses with transportation.

The locomotive was waiting for them as Adams reined in and dropped from his saddle. He nodded at the high-sided flatbed trucks which would provide his men's mounts with a much-needed rest. But he would not venture aboard the train he had hired. For Adams had never liked the great iron horses whose tracks had carved up the once pristine ranges and brought untold amounts of human vermin from the distant East. The trains served a purpose, but he had vowed never actually to ride on one. If his bones hurt, that was something he would endure. It reminded him how hard he had worked.

He inhaled deeply and smiled as he took off his brand-new black ten-gallon hat. He beat the dust from its wide brim against his leather chaps and then glanced at his oldest friend, the bearded Tomahawk.

'You gonna get up on that thing, old-timer?'

Tomahawk liked the idea of not sleeping on the trail, but like his pal, did not take to the large steam-snorting inventions.

'Not willingly, Gene.'

Adams laughed and watched as his men dismounted all around him. The bearded Tomahawk carefully slid off his saddle and walked around vainly trying to straighten his legs.

'Go on, boys.' Adams raised his voice. 'Get them horses up on the flatbeds and unsaddle the critters. There's feed and water up there for them. When you've done that, you can go and find where your bunks are in them mighty fine-looking cars.'

'Ain't you coming on the train with us, Gene?' Happy Summers asked as he stroked the dusty nose of his buckskin gelding.

Adams laughed again and patted his faithful mount.

'Nope. I'm taking the trail south back to the Bar 10 on old Amy.'

'Why, Gene?' Rip Calloway asked. 'Ya spent all that money hiring the train and you're gonna ride ya horse home.'

'Never liked trains, boys.' Adams shrugged. 'I like riding my old horse just like I've always done. But you boys have all worked hard and you deserve a rest.'

The faces of the Bar 10 cowboys looked sheepishly at one another. They were tired but also felt guilty that they would be taking the easy way home whilst their boss would be roughing it on the trail.

Happy frowned and spoke for the rest of the cowboys.

'I don't like the idea of us sleeping in a soft bed when you're out there on the trail, Gene.'

Tomahawk scratched his beard.

'I'll be with ya, Gene. Just like the old days. Reckon Johnny will cotton to a nice ride too.'

Adams smiled. His tanned features highlighted the white hair that fringed his still-handsome face.

'Tomahawk will still be with me, boys.' He nodded. 'Just as always. We've ridden harder trails than the one I've got planned for us.'

Rip Calloway moved closer to the rancher.

'What about the cattle money, Gene? You taking all that money on the trail with you?'

'Yep,' Adams answered firmly. 'I sure

ain't putting it on that train. Trains get robbed by folks like Jesse James and other such trash.'

'It's safer with me and Gene, ya young whipper-snapper.' The ancient Tomahawk smiled toothlessly. 'Besides, we'll have young Johnny with us if we do get into trouble.'

'Where is Johnny?' Adams asked. His blue eyes darted around the faces of the assembled cowboys. 'I thought he was with us when we headed out of McCoy.'

'He was with us until he saw that sweet little gal,' Rip said with a raise of an eyebrow.

'Which gal was that?' Adams asked.

'Oh, it was just that Peggy Smith, Gene,' Tomahawk ventured.

'No it weren't Peggy at all, Tomahawk,' Happy corrected. 'It was the other one. Sue something or other.'

Gene Adams gave a wide grin and shrugged. He then led his horse to a trough next to the long train. The animal dropped its head and started to drink.

'Go on, boys. Get them horses unsaddled and up on to that flatbed. Times a-wasting.'

One of the Bar 10's newest recruits was a tall, thin figure with a toothpick always stuck in the corner of his mouth. His name was Red Hawke. He had a low drawl and a loose manner which had endeared him to the rest of the Bar 10 cowboys since he had been hired by Adams. He moved slowly up to the rancher and removed his hat.

'Can I come with you boys, boss?' he asked bashfully. 'I'm kinda not used to trains myself. I'm a mite scared of the darn things.'

Adams looked at the man who seemed to be all legs and arms topped by a crimson tuft of hair. It was hard not to smile when you faced Hawke.

'Well, I ain't sure, Red,' Adams teased. 'Do you reckon you can handle another couple of weeks eating Tomahawk's cooking?'

Red blushed and glanced at the crusty old-timer.

'I done thought Tomahawk's vittles was an awful lot like my old ma's.'

Tomahawk's eyebrows rose as he smiled.

'This boy is real Bar 10, Gene. Ya gotta let him ride with us. He's got sophisticated taste-buds there.'

'OK, Red. You can ride with us.' Adams laughed.

'Gee, thanks.' Red Hawke ambled back to his mount and led it to the water-trough.

Tomahawk rested his bony hip on the edge of the trough and watched as his black horse drank.

'Here comes Johnny now, Gene.'

Adams turned and saw the plume of dust rise. Then he saw the young rider standing in his stirrups as he clung to his reins. The pinto galloped towards them.

'He'll never learn, Gene.' Tomahawk sniffed. 'That ain't no way to treat a horse.'

'What you mean, Tomahawk?' Adams rested a boot on the weathered wooden side of the trough.

'He'll kill that pinto making it run at that speed.'

Gene grabbed the older man's beard and tugged it.

'Since Johnny has had that pony of his, you've had three horses all end up dead.'

Tomahawk squinted up at the smiling rancher.

'That was different, son. All my horses got shot out from under me. Ya can't blame me for that.'

'Ever wondered why so many folks shoot at you?' Adams laughed. 'Maybe they're trying to tell you something. Them poor horses being stuck underneath a human target like you. It's a crying shame.'

'Ah, shut ya trap,' Tomahawk flustered. 'The only reason I've had folks shoot at me is coz I was saving your worthless hide.'

Gene Adams turned and watched as his riders slowly started to lead their horses up the ramps on to the flatbeds.

Johnny Puma thundered across the flat range astride his pony and only hauled rein when he was right next to the thoughtful rancher. Dust drifted off the pinto's hoofs over his pals. Johnny grinned broadly at the rest of the cowboys.

'I caught ya all up darn quick, huh?'

'I reckons we're looking at the cat that got the cream, Gene.' Tomahawk winked at the rancher.

'What you gabbing about, old-timer?' Johnny asked. He tapped his spurs into his pony and trotted alongside the water-trough.

Gene put his hat back on and gave the youngster a knowing smile.

'So did little Sue Green give you a few kisses, Johnny?'

Johnny blushed.

'Shucks, Gene. What ya trying to say?'

'We know that you got kinda side-tracked when we was leaving town.' Adams nodded. 'We reckoned that little Sue was just all puckered up and you just had to help the poor child. Ain't that right, boys?'

The rest of the cowboys all agreed at once.

'You must be darn tuckered, Johnny.' Tomahawk giggled. 'That Sue is a mighty fit gal. Reckon she could hold her own in a wrestlin'-match.'

'Sometimes I just think ya all jealous,' Johnny said. He pulled his hat-brim down to cover his inflamed cheeks.

'Damn right we're all jealous, ya young pup.' Tomahawk winked again. 'All the gals that used to take a shine to me are all dead now.'

'Did she taste as good as she looks, son?' Gene asked. 'As good as apple pie?'

Johnny gave a belly laugh.

'Yep. With brown sugar and cinnamon on top.'

Happy Summers gave a howl.

'That's good. Darn good.'

Johnny threw his right leg over his pony's neck and dropped down beside his pals. He gave Happy a quick glance.

'You'd have eaten her, Happy.'

'Reckon so.' The rotund wrangler nodded. 'What a darn great meal though.'

Johnny looped his reins around the saddle horn of Tomahawk's gelding and stepped next to Adams.

'How come you ain't got your horses on the train yet, Gene?'

Adams eyed the youngster.

'I ain't going on the train, Johnny. Don't you recall me telling you? I thought that you, Tomahawk and me would take us a nice peaceful ride home instead.'

'Red's comin' with us too.' Tomahawk smiled. 'Darn nice boy is young Red. Not like some tumble-weeds I could name.'

Johnny removed his Stetson and used his bandanna to clean the dust from his handsome features.

'Oh, yeah, Gene. I remember you saying something about us riding home and not taking the train.'

'No ya don't remember Gene tellin' ya,' Tomahawk said, his tongue rotating around his whiskers. 'Ya just trying to look smart, Johnny.'

Johnny rested his hands on his gun grips and watched the last of the horses being led up on to the flatbed. He glanced at Adams.

'Seems like a waste of money letting the boys take the train when we gotta ride.'

Gene Adams grinned.

'You can take the train, Johnny. It ain't no skin off my nose if'n you think the ride will be a tad too tough for you.'

Johnny tilted his head.

'Which way you heading?'

'We was thinking of going by Sutter's Corner,' Adams said knowing that a few years earlier the youngster had fallen for the hotel owner's daughter there. 'You do recall Sutter's Corner, don't you, Johnny?'

The cowboy smiled broadly.

'I recall a certain Nancy Davis, Gene.'

34

Tomahawk stood and scratched his sides.

'I recall we run into big trouble there, boys. Lost me a horse as I remember.'

'You're always losing horses some-place,' Adams noted.

'Hey!' Tomahawk scratched his beard. 'Is that the place where there was ghosts?'

Adams sighed.

'They weren't real ghosts, old-timer. They were thieves.'

'Oh yeah.' Tomahawk nodded as his tongue traced across his open mouth.

'For all we know the hotel is closed up now, Gene,' Johnny said thought-fully. 'The rest of the place was a ghost town back then. Chances are the hotel is just a ruin now.'

'If it is, we'll just have to make camp,' Adams said. The rest of his Bar 10 riders carefully locked the doors to the flatbed cars. He walked to the cowboys and beamed a broad smile at them.

'You sure you ain't coming with us, Gene?' Rip asked.

Gene rested his gloved knuckles on

his famed golden guns.

'You know something? I'm mighty proud of you boys. You have yourselves a good rest. See you all back on the Bar 10.'

Adams nodded to the attendant, who waved his flag to the engineer of the massive locomotive.

'See ya back on the Bar 10, Gene,' Happy called out.

'You be careful, boys,' Rip added.

The locomotive whistle blew. The train slowly moved along its gleaming rails as smoke billowed from its black stack. The four horsemen watched until it had disappeared in the distance and only grey smoke remained hanging on the crisp air.

Gene patted Hawke's high, lean shoulder.

'Get yourself mounted, Red.'

The awkward youngster nodded and did as he was told.

Gene Adams gathered his reins, then stepped into his stirrup. He glided up on top of the tall mare. There was a steely look in the rancher's blue eyes.

'Ready to ride?' Adams asked.

Johnny threw himself up on to his pony.

'Yep.'

'Ya darn tootin', I'm ready,' Tomahawk said. He gripped his horse's mane and mounted. 'I've bin waiting for hours for you two old women to stop gossiping.'

The riders of the Bar 10 spurred.

4

The six ruthless riders had thundered up through the hills above the rail spur long before Adams or any of his men had reached the awaiting locomotive. The outlaws knew that the land beyond this place was one of total contrasts. Well-nourished brush between every huge golden coloured boulder dominated everything for a score of miles until the trail reached the ghost town of Sutter's Corner. Beyond the virtually abandoned settlement the land became as dry as a desert beneath high dusty crags. It was no surprise to anyone who had ridden this trail that it was called Devil's Canyon. To the east, a huge mountain range rose defiantly up out of the heat-haze into the heavens.

That was the place which had saved the lives of countless unwary drifters who had steered their mounts towards it over the years. A small fresh-water lake lay surrounded by well-nourished trees, almost hidden from the arid land beyond. The lake was fed by a waterfall that cascaded from fifty feet above it.

Besides knowing about the land towards which the Bar 10 riders had headed, Samson Stone had also learned a lot about Adams well before he had led his deadly gang out of McCoy. Stone had extracted so much information concerning Gene Adams that although he had been told of the train which had been hired to take Adams's loyal cowboys back to Texas, the outlaw was certain Gene Adams would not be on it.

High amongst the trees, Samson Stone smiled broadly when his theory was proved correct. The six outlaws had waited for nearly two hours up in the densely wooded hills, waiting for the riders of the Bar 10 to arrive at the rail spur. The train had been there even before Stone had reined in ahead of his gang after their ride from McCoy.

The outlaw leader had never been known for his patience and the long wait had made Stone anxious. He rested a hand against a tall sapling and chewed on the butt of an unlit cigar. He nodded silently as the four Bar 10 horsemen eventually headed off towards Sutter's Corner and Devil's Canyon.

'How did ya know that Adams would not get on that train, Samson?' a sweat-soaked Talbot asked.

'I know Gene Adams better than he knows himself,' Stone muttered under his breath.

Poke Green moved close to the thoughtful Stone. He grinned and then leaned close to the outlaw leader.

'Ya just got lucky, Samson. Admit it, ya sidewinder. Ya just got lucky,' he mocked jokingly.

There was something in his tone of the voice that angered Stone. It was as if a stick of dynamite had suddenly had its fuse lit. Stone swiftly grabbed at Green's bandanna. His strong hand looped the bandanna around his wrist several times until his knuckles were pressed into the stunned outlaw's throat. He tightened his grip even more and watched Green's eyes bulge.

'You got a big mouth there, Poke. Too damn big.'

There was a desperation in the face of the choking outlaw as Stone raised his arm. Green was almost on the toes of his cowboy boots. Green's fingers clawed at the gloved hand beneath the snarling face.

'What's that you was saying, Poke?' Stone taunted the choking figure. 'What's that ya trying to say?'

The other outlaws realized that the strange insanity which Samson Stone concealed so well most of the time was still there, simmering unseen below the self-righteous façade which the outlaw leader had created for himself. His free hand drew a gun from its holster and cocked its hammer, then lifted the heavy weapon until its barrel rested against Green's cheek-bone.

'I'm gonna blow ya head clean off

41

those shoulders of yours, Poke,' Stone whispered.

'Samson!' Zon Mooney raised his voice just enough to catch the attention of the crazed Stone.

Stone looked across at Mooney and then at the helpless man he was strangling. Eventually as he saw Green's face change colour, he released his grip. Green staggered and then felt the full force of Stone's gun grip catch him high on the side of his head. Green fell to the ground as Stone lashed out with his right boot. A trail of blood sprayed from the outlaw's mouth. Poke Green rolled over and over until he reached the other seated outlaws. They helped the bleeding man up and sat him on his saddle.

Samson Stone glared at them and pointed with his gun.

'Nobody makes fun of me. Understand? I'd have used this gun if Adams and his cowboys weren't so close.'

The outlaws nodded and mumbled in unison.

Stone inhaled deeply and holstered the Colt. As quickly as his temper had risen to explosive levels, it fell back to normal. It was as if nothing had happened. He moved to the men who were sitting in a circle on their saddles. Then he lowered himself down and then struck a match with his thumbnail. When the flame flared he tossed it on to the dried kindling and moss they had gathered earlier. The fire lit quickly. Stone then carefully placed a handful of logs over the flames.

'How did I know Gene Adams would not take the train? I looked and I listened,' Stone said in a low raspy voice.

'Yeah?' Chard raised an eyebrow. 'What does that mean?'

Stone picked up a smouldering stick and touched the tip of his cigar. He sucked in the smoke, then tossed the stick back into the flames.

'To start with, I knew some rich *hombre* was headed to McCoy with a sizable herd of steers, Leroy,' Stone mumbled, and drew more acrid smoke into his lungs. 'I had to find out his name. I learned that by looking and listening. Right?'

'Right.' Chard nodded.

'I then had to find out how this rancher was going back to his cattle spread after he'd been paid for his herd,' Stone continued. 'I did that by hanging around Adams and his men in the saloon and other places they visited. One of them places was the train depot.'

Zon Mooney placed a large skillet on top of the flames.

'I don't get it.'

'Adams booked a train for his cowboys and their horses at the depot,' Stone said. He pulled the twisted weed from his mouth and exhaled the smoke. 'I heard him telling the clerk at the depot that he would not be takin' that train himself coz he don't cotton to trains.'

'Did you know that them other three cowboys would be riding with him away from here, Samson?' Carson Farmer asked.

'I figured the old-timer would stay with Adams coz folks said that the two critters are glued at the hip.' Stone nodded. 'I guessed the youngster on the pinto pony would also stay with the rancher. Lots of folks in McCoy said that he's like a son to the big Bar 10 man. I reckoned on them all sticking close to one another. The long-legged redhead was a surprise though. I didn't figure on him riding with them.'

Mooney unwrapped a roll of greased paper and pulled out a dozen slices of salt bacon and a lump of fat. He dropped it all on to the large pan. It started to spit and sizzle.

'Ya figure we got us time to eat this grub, Samson?' he asked.

Stone smiled and dropped the cigar butt on to the flames.

'We've got plenty of time, Zon,' he said through a cloud of smoke. 'I know them hills like the back of my hand and there ain't no point in us bushwhacking them until they get to Devil's Canyon, a few miles beyond Sutter's Corner. That'll take days.'

'I heard me a few things about Gene Adams too, when we was in McCoy, Samson.' Talbot sighed heavily.

'What kinda things?' Stone asked.

'I heard tell that he is a living legend, Samson.' Talbot gulped. 'He got them golden guns and he's darned good at killing with them.'

'I've heard things about Adams as well.' Stone smiled. 'He got a weakness that will be the death of him. A soft spot.'

'What ya mean?' Farmer asked.

'The old-timer and the kid on the pinto are as close as kin to Adams.' Stone said. 'We have to get them and then Adams will be willing to hand over every damn gold piece he's got to have them set free.'

Mooney shook the skillet and pushed the bacon around with a Bowie knife.

'Adams would hand over all his money just to have them critters set free?' he questioned.

'Yep.' Stone nodded.

'Are ya sure about that, Samson?'

Samson Stone gritted his teeth.

'Damn sure, Zon!'

'Is that coz you spent so much time looking and listening back in McCoy?' Farmer chipped in.

'Yep!'

The men inhaled the smell of the frying bacon and tried to relax. It was impossible with a man like Samson Stone sitting so close. They each looked at the stunned, bleeding Poke Green who swayed amid them. They all knew that Stone was capable of doing much worse should he be so inclined.

Stone had a way of making even the most hardened of souls fear for their lives.

'When do we ride?' Chard asked.

'A tad before sundown,' Stone answered. 'We'll ride all night and get a few miles ahead of the varmints before they even get out of their bedrolls. The trick is for Adams and his pals not to have any idea that they've got company up in them hills. Once we're ahead of them, we stay there until it's time.'

'Time for what?' a dazed Poke Green asked through bloodied teeth.

Stone kicked out again and caught the outlaw in his groin.

'Pay attention,' he snarled.

5

They had not travelled through this landscape for more than three years, yet once it had been the favoured trail home to Texas for all cattle drovers, especially the Bar 10. The hills were a mixture of gigantic golden boulders and green brush. Dark broad-leafed trees hung over narrow trails giving much needed shade to all who ventured to this remote place. It was now more overgrown than it had once been, yet Gene Adams recognized every inch of the twisting route along which he used to travel twice a year back to the famed Bar 10.

Dust drifted off the highest peaks, which somehow managed to rise above the dark-green tree canopies into the cloudless blue sky. The sun was low and each of the four horsemen knew that it would set within the hour. Adams and his trio of companions had made good progress up the twisting trail but there were limits even to their stamina.

Gene Adams leaned back and reined in. The mare slowed to a stop, as did the other horses. Adams looked around them before dismounting.

'Reckon this is as good a place as any for us to make camp, boys,' Adams said. He dropped his reins and allowed his chestnut mare to graze on the long grass which grew under every tree on the trail. 'Well sheltered from the breeze that can come off them buttes.'

'Now ya talkin', Gene.' Tomahawk leaned over his horse's neck and dragged his tired right leg over his saddle cantle. He dismounted and shook his weary head. 'I'm as stiff as a baker's board.'

Adams walked up to his tired pal and tugged hard at the man's jutting beard.

'You might be getting old, Toma-hawk.'

The oldest of the Bar 10 riders chuckled and found a rock to sit down on. His wrinkled eyes darted all around them. It was as if he felt that they were not alone in this remote place. He rose, stood bow-legged and squinted up at the high ground which surrounded them.

'Hey! You figure that there might be critters up in these hills, Gene?'

Adams lifted the left fender and hooked the stirrup over the silver-embossed saddle horn. He glanced around at Tomahawk.

'What you mean, old-timer?'

Tomahawk rubbed his neck.

'I just got me a feeling, boy. Ya know what I mean?'

Adams's blue eyes stared from beneath the black brim of his ten-gallon hat all around the brush which towered over them. He knew that the old-timer had lived with Indians during his early life and had become the best tracker he had ever known. Tomahawk had learned a lot from his Indian friends and one of those things was how to feel trouble in his bones.

'You reckon there might be some-thing or someone out there in the hills, Tomahawk?' Adams asked quietly so that their two young pals could not hear.

The old man squinted at Adams.

'I ain't sure. I just got me a feeling in my craw.'

Adams looked all around them at the trees which cast long shadows as the sun got lower in the sky.

'I reckon you might be right. I noticed that there ain't been many birds singing since we left the rail tracks. Like something spooked them.'

Johnny Puma and Red Hawke dismounted.

'What you saying there, Gene?' Johnny asked. He led his long-legged pal towards the two men.

'Me and old Tomahawk was saying that there ain't been a lot of birds singing, son.'

Johnny grinned wide and looked at Red.

'The old folks want the birds to sing, Red.'

'Yeah?' Hawke shrugged.

'Me and Red could sing ya a few songs.'

Adams continued to unbuckle his cinch straps, then he hauled the heavy saddle off the mare's back. He dropped it down next to Johnny's feet.

'You gotta ask yourself why the birds ain't singing, Johnny.'

The smile left Johnny's face.

'What ya mean, Gene?'

Tomahawk shook his head in frustration.

'Ain't I learned ya nothing, boy? Birds stop singing when they've been disturbed.'

'Like seeing four dust-caked cowboys riding towards them?' Johnny asked. 'I reckon they spotted us and just took flight.'

'Yep. But listen up, there ain't one of them singing anywhere around us. There might be something out there in the brush that's scared them.'

Johnny looked around the hills. Trees and wild brush covered the huge boulders so that it was impossible to see anything clearly. His eyes darted back to the old man.

'Are there bears or mountain lions around here?'

Tomahawk nodded and gave a toothless grin.

'Ya darn tootin', Johnny. Big 'uns.'

Johnny marched up to Adams. There was genuine concern etched in his youthful features.

'I thought all the critters around here were wiped out years ago, Gene. Now old gummy here reckons that there are bears and lions out there. Well?'

Adams nodded.

'They were wiped out, son. But that was when this old trail was busy with scores of folks like us headed home. It's been a long time since men rode these trails regular and when the men leave a chunk of land alone, the animals return.'

'Bears?' Red gulped. 'I ain't partial to meeting no bears, boss. They eats folks.'

Adams chuckled.

'Don't fret, Red. Bears tend to like their meals with a mite more meat on their bones than you've got.'

Tomahawk stood and ambled to his horse.

'Might not be bears and lions. It might be two-legged critters, boys,' he said knowingly. 'Bushwhackin' varmints.'

'Yeah?' Johnny loosened his bandanna and swallowed.

'Yeah!' Tomahawk replied. 'Birds are more scared of two legged-critters than they are of bears and lions.'

'You still want to make camp here, Gene?' Johnny asked the tall rancher.

Adams surveyed the brush.

'Yep. We'll make camp here. A nice big fire will keep anything on four legs away. If there are men out there, they can't sneak up on us here. Well, not easily anyway.'

Tomahawk pulled his saddle and blanket off the horse and dropped them at his feet. He patted the horse's neck, then turned to the two youngest members of their group.

'Get some kindling, you young whippersnappers. I'm gonna cook us up some vittles.'

Johnny and Red moved nervously away.

'We'll get us a whole bunch of kindling, Tomahawk,' Johnny said.

As the two young cowboys started to search for dry kindling, Tomahawk walked to Adams's side. He noticed the rancher was thoughtful.

'I might be just imagining things, Gene. Could be these old bones are starting to creak so much I'm confusing being tuckered with somethin' else.'

'I've been thinking about when we were back in McCoy,' Adams said. 'Did you notice that we kept bumping into the same few men wherever we were?'

'Who ya talkin' about?' Tomahawk shrugged.

'There was one man in particular. I seen him at the auctioneer's office and in the saloon. I've not seen him before.' The rancher sighed. 'Didn't strike me at the time. Now it seems a little odd.'

'Ya just tired, boy.' Tomahawk winked.

Adams pulled one of his golden Colts from its holster and checked that there was a fresh bullet in each of its six chambers.

'I'm still going to take me a little walk around to have a look. We ain't got nothing to lose by being cautious.'

'Be careful, boy.'

'Rustle up them vittles, Tomahawk.' Adams tugged the older man's beard again and turned. He cocked the golden hammer, then started up into the brush.

'Where's Gene going, Tomahawk?' Red asked innocently.

'Just keep hunting that kindling, sonny.' Tomahawk opened up his saddle-bags and pulled out a small, blackened coffee-pot and a well-used pan. 'He'll be back!'

★   ★   ★

Gene Adams moved like a man of half his years through the black shadows around the camp. He held the golden Colt ahead of him as he negotiated the mixture of rocks, trees and bushes. The rancher moved surprisingly quietly for a big man. His every instinct was honed like a straight razor, looking for something that might pose a danger to his three cowboys and himself.

His mind was filled with questions.

Had someone back at McCoy decided to try their luck?

Were the saddle-bags filled with gold coins too much of a temptation to some worthless varmint?

He had been robbed in these hills before.

Would fate repeat itself?

Suddenly his flared nostrils caught the scent of something drifting on the air over him. Adams stopped and rested against a big boulder twice his own height and tried to focus through the half-light up into the untamed wilderness.

Then he looked down into the clearing. He could see the camp-fire blazing through the trees and dense bushes as Tomahawk prepared their supper.

Was it the aroma of the old-timer's cooking over the fire that had drifted up into the brush?

There was no way of telling for sure. He continued on up over the rocks and around the bushes until he had circled his friends below him.

Adams fought through the tangled brush that made it almost impossible to keep going. At last he was convinced that even a lizard would have trouble making its way down through this web of sharp thorns which filled most of the gaps between the gigantic boulders. Anything larger had no chance.

He knew that this was no place for an ambush. The ground was too uneven for anyone to venture down with any guarantee of success.

After more than twenty minutes, the rancher returned to the three cowboys sitting around the camp-fire.

'Well?' a crouching Tomahawk asked

as he stirred a skillet full of beans with a ladle. 'Ya find anything up there, boy?'

Gene Adams released the hammer on his gun, holstered the weapon and moved to the roaring fire. His eyes looked on each of the men in turn.

'Ain't no way that anything could make their way down through that brush, boys.' Adams sighed.

'Ya shirt-sleeve's torn, Gene.' Johnny pointed.

'Yep. It's mighty rough out there.' Adams nodded and sat down next to Tomahawk. 'Don't go fretting about any critters getting the drop on us. They'd be skinned alive just trying.'

'Have some beans, boy.' Tomahawk handed a tin plate to the rancher and piled it high.

Adams accepted a spoon, scooped up some beans and placed them in his mouth. He chewed, then raised an eyebrow and looked at the old-timer.

'These beans are kinda soapy.'

Tomahawk's wrinkled eyes sparkled in the moonlight as he grinned.

'Proves I washed the plates, don't it?'

'Yep.' Adams smiled. 'Can't fault you for having dirty plates, old-timer.'

'They do taste a tad soapy.' Johnny agreed with the rancher opposite him.

Tomahawk tossed a bag of salt at Johnny.

'Here, ya young whippersnapper. Put some salt on 'em.'

'My beans taste real fine. Just like my ma makes,' Red said. He scooped up the last of his meal and devoured them. 'I'd like me some more.'

'I like that boy, Gene.' Tomahawk winked as he ladled some more of the bubbling beans on to the long-legged cowboy's tin plate. 'He knows good vittles when he tastes them. Not like some folks around here.'

Adams did not say another word. He just kept chewing and thinking about the faces he recalled back in McCoy. Faces of men who, on reflection, seemed too darned interested in him.

Him or the golden coins in his saddle-bags.

6

Darkness had overwhelmed the rolling hills like a blanket. A million stars and a half-moon illuminated the weathered wooden structures in a bluish eerie light. A howling coyote high in the hills competed with countless unseen crickets down on the dry dusty ground.

It was another evening exactly the same as so many which had gone before in this desolate place.

Yet it had not always been like this. The town of Sutter's Corner had once been a thriving community set amid a landscape of mountains boulders and tall dark trees. Times changed quickly in the old West.

Like so many similar towns, Sutter's Corner had grown quickly and died with equal speed. No sooner had the last building been constructed than the decline started. New trails, which shortened the time back to Texas, reduced the flood of passing traffic to a mere trickle. Within a decade only a ghost town remained, playing host to tumbleweed and a multitude of creatures seeking sanctuary from the often brutal elements.

Yet Sutter's Corner was not truly dead.

A spark of life still glowed out in the wilderness amid the wreckage.

A solitary building defied the ruins which surrounded it and lit its welcoming lanterns each and every night. Most evenings it was a futile exercise, but sometimes it managed to draw human moths to its flames.

Amid the desolation which Sutter's Corner had become, the hotel still remained defiantly open. Few people ever travelled this route any longer, but those who did managed to make the hotel still profitable.

As was his usual habit, the hotel-owner, known to one and all as Old Man Davis, walked out on his porch to enjoy a pipeful of tobacco. He would remain watching and waiting for someone to head towards his hotel, seeking a cooked meal and a bed for the night, until it grew too cold. Only then would he return to his roaring log-fire and admit defeat for another day.

The two riders who guided their mounts through the dusty streets of the ghostly buildings had seen the lantern-light a mile or so down the trail. They had instinctively steered their horses towards it.

But these were two horsemen whom most people would have preferred not to encounter at all.

Old Man Davis stood on the hotel porch and stared through the eerie blue moonlight at the approaching riders. He rubbed his chin thoughtfully.

'We got us some guests by the looks of it, Nancy honey,' the old man called over his shoulder.

A beautiful female came out through the open doors and stood next to her uncle. The hotel was perched far higher up than the rest of the ghost town and offered unchallenged views of every one of the decaying buildings.

'I wonder who they are?' she whispered as if the distant men could hear her.

'Don't matter none, girl,' Davis said. 'Go and make sure we got two rooms ready for guests. They might cotton to a soft bed rather than another night under them stars.'

'I'll check number one and two.' Nancy turned on her heel and rushed back into the hotel.

Davis nodded and pulled out a corncob pipe. He placed its stem between his teeth and chewed on it. The riders were in no hurry to reach the well-illuminated hotel. They just allowed their horses to walk straight down the centre of the wide, abandoned street.

Davis ran a match down a wooden upright and put its flame an inch above his pipe bowl. He sucked it into the fresh tobacco and puffed as the riders drew closer.

'Welcome!' Davis called out with a hand-gesture.

One of the horsemen leaned back slightly as their mounts started up the rise towards the hotel.

He dragged his long-barrelled Winchester from its scabbard beneath the saddle and cranked its mechanism. The whole operation was fluid and well practised. It had taken a mere heartbeat to complete.

The hotel-owner pulled the pipe from his mouth and wondered why he was suddenly looking down the barrel of the deadly rifle.

'What's going on?' Davis asked as both riders drew rein and stopped their horses below him. 'Why you aiming that carbine at me, boy?'

'He's asking what's wrong, Clem.' Ethan Swift chuckled as he removed his battered hat and stared across at his younger brother.

'I heard him, Ethan.' Clem Swift smiled as he rested the wooden rifle stock against his middle. 'Damned if I don't feel kinda upset at him talking to us like that.'

'He's also a nosy old critter.'

'Yep. Can't stand nosy critters.' Clem Swift nodded in agreement.

The old man wanted to turn and run, but his legs refused to obey his mind. Davis hesitated. He had no idea whether it was wiser to flee or remain rooted to the spot below his porch overhang. In all his days, he had never had anyone aim a weapon at him.

'If you boys are thinking of robbing me, it's hardly worth you wasting sweat. All I got is eighteen dollars in silver coin in the desk drawer.'

'A tidy sum.' Clem Swift nodded.

'That's sixteen dollars more than we got, Clem.' Ethan nodded.

Davis could not comprehend the two riders' motives. Were they serious or just a pair of young drifters who liked to play jokes on the old?

'C . . . come on now, boys. You've had your fun. Put that rifle down. You can have the money. I ain't gonna stop you. But don't shoot.' That was the first time Davis had begged for anything in his long life.

It made no difference at all.

The outlaw called Clem squeezed the trigger.

A blinding flash lit up the darkness. The sound of the rifle-shot was deafening.

Davis was lifted off his feet by the sheer force of the rifle bullet and sent crashing into the front wall of the hotel. A trail of blood was smeared over the wall as the limp body slipped down on to the wooden decking.

The deadly sound echoed for minutes around the ghost town. It was only drowned out by the chilling laughter of the lethal horsemen.

7

Acrid gunsmoke hung on the night air over the hotel porch. Clem Swift dismounted carefully with the smoking Winchester still in his right hand. He cranked its mechanism again and looked all around them as his brother slowly eased himself off the back of his lathered-up mount.

'That was so damn easy, Ethan.' Clem laughed. 'I swear some folks are just plain stupid.'

'Quiet.' Ethan ordered. He stepped up on to the porch, then took two steps and stood in the pool of blood that had spread out from Davis's lifeless body. His emotionless eyes watched the red gore as it trailed along the wooden boards and started to drip off the porch.

Clem did as he was told and remained by their horses, silently listening out for the sound of others. He heard nothing except the stridulation of noisy crickets which buzzed all around the hotel and ghost town.

'He sure had a lot of blood for a skinny old critter,' Ethan noted. He walked towards the open hotel doorway and stared inside.

Clem joined his brother.

'Reckon there's more folks around here, Ethan?'

'Hard to tell.' Ethan marched in across the well-worn carpet and headed straight to the hotel desk. He moved around it and dragged every drawer open until he found the one with the silver dollars. He scooped them up and forced them down into his pants pocket.

'Half of them silver dollars is mine, Ethan,' Clem pointed out. 'I shot the old buzzard.'

Ethan nodded, yet he did not share their pitiful blood-money with his trigger-happy sibling. He looked into the large dining-area and then to the parlour with its roaring fire in the heart of the black-leaded mantel.

'Ya gonna give me a share of that money?' Clem asked again. His hands were gripping the Winchester rifle firmly across his chest.

The elder brother dismissed the question and then made his way back into the lobby. His eyes glanced down at the bloody footprints they had left over the wide expanse of floor.

'Hush up,' Ethan said as he looked up at the ceiling above the hotel lobby. His eyes narrowed on the flaking plaster. 'Did ya hear that?'

'What?'

'Did you hear something upstairs?' Ethan spat at the floor and the palm of his right hand stroked the gun hammer that jutted from its holster. 'I thought I heard something.'

'Reckon there's somebody up there?' Clem held the rifle away from his body.

'What are the odds that one old man would be all the ways out here on his lonesome in a big hotel?' Ethan asked.

He drew his gun and cocked its hammer. 'Stands to reason that he'd need help to run this place.'

Clem looked towards the staircase.

'Maybe we should head on up them stairs and take us a good look-see?'

Ethan Swift was not as foolhardy as his brother.

'What if there's a couple of men up there with guns? We'd not even make the landing.'

'You reckon?' Clem aimed his rifle at the stairs and edged closer to his brother.

'You want to end up like that old man out there?' Ethan pointed at the porch with the thumb of his left hand.

'Nope.' Clem was confused. 'But how are we gonna find out if'n we don't go and take us a look-see?'

Ethan smiled. It was not the smile of someone who was happy. It was the cunning smile of a man who knew every dirty trick in the unwritten book used by the saddle tramps who wondered aimlessly through the Wild

West, leaving a trail of blood in their wake.

'C'mon!' he said turning back towards the open door. 'I got me a plan.'

Both men marched out on to the porch and dropped down into the moonlight. They gathered up their reins, then mounted their lathered-up horses. Ethan winked at his brother, who grinned in reply.

'Let's ride!' Ethan shouted out at the top of his voice.

They turned their horses and spurred hard. Both horses galloped up towards the trail that led to Devil's Canyon. Dust raised by the hoofs of their horses hung on the evening air.

For more than five minutes the terrified female had waited upstairs until she was confident that the two riders had actually ridden away from the hotel.

A shaking Nancy Davis slowly descended the wide staircase into the hotel lobby. She had heard the shot and knew in her heart that her uncle had been the target. Nancy stared in horror at the bloody boot-prints which showed where the two men had walked after they had unleashed their venom on the innocent old man. She made her way across the wide lobby until she reached the open doorway.

For a few seemingly endless seconds she hovered, unable either to move ahead or to go back. It was as if she were frozen.

Inhaling deeply, she summoned up every ounce of her courage and stepped out on to the porch.

The sight that greeted her beautiful eyes was so horrible that she felt herself moving backward as if drawn by invisible strings. The solid wall stopped her retreat. Nancy closed her eyes and pushed both hands over her mouth as every sinew in her slim body trembled.

She wanted to scream, but knew that that would be too dangerous. The putrid taste of bile filled her throat and mouth, but she refused to be sick.

Nancy opened her eyes. Her worst fears were realized.

Tears streamed down over her pale, lantern-lit features as she tried to steady herself.

Nancy knew that there was little doubt that her uncle was dead but there was only one way to be certain.

She took a step forward and then knelt down. The still warm blood soaked into her blue dress as her tiny fingers vainly searched her uncle's body for any sign of life.

A faint pulse was all she needed to know that he was not dead, as the two riders had believed. Yet no matter how much she checked his neck or blood-soaked chest, she could not find the beat of a living heart.

Davis was dead.

Suddenly she heard something behind her beside the edge of the porch steps. It was the cackle of the two grinning Swift brothers. Her eyes widened in shock.

'Look what we caught, Clem!'

'A real pretty one.'

'I ain't ever set eyes on nothing as pretty!'

'But she's a witness!'

'And we kills witnesses!'

Before Nancy could rise to her feet, the two men had rushed at her. They were far too powerful for her. She felt their filthy hands on her right wrist and ankle. They were strong. Too strong. The two men dragged her off the boardwalk as if she were a rag-doll.

She landed heavily at their feet.

Ethan bent over and slapped her with all his might. Blood trickled from the corner of her mouth.

'Why?' she gasped. 'Why did you kill my poor uncle, you dirty heathens? Why? He never did you any harm. He never hurt no one in all his days. Why did you kill him?'

They stood over her.

Their laughter chilled her bruised soul.

'Why not, girl?' Clem asked her with a surprised expression etched on his face. 'Why shouldn't we have killed him? He weren't no kin to us.'

Nancy lay on her back knowing that

the two men above her lived their lives by a very different set of morals than most of those she had encountered in her short life.

'You killed him because he wasn't related to you?'

Ethan Swift bent down and grabbed her face with his strong fingers. He squeezed hard.

'Don't you know nothing, girl? You kill or you gets killed in these parts! Only the strong survive! Folks like us wouldn't last too long if'n we felt sorry for the vermin we bumps into!'

Clem levelled the rifle barrel at her head.

'Should I kill her, Ethan?' he asked. 'I ought to blow her head off her shoulders!'

Ethan Swift stared down at the helpless female and licked his lips. He had other ideas for her.

'Not yet, Clem. I reckon we could get us some fun out of this girl. She might serve her purpose for the next couple of weeks.'

Clem Swift smiled broadly and raised his rifle until its long barrel rested on his shoulder.

'I get ya meaning.'

Nancy felt a cold shiver trace over her as she realized what the two men meant. She tried to move but Ethan placed his boot on her blonde hair. She was trapped.

'Let me go!' she whispered angrily.

'We will when we're finished with you, girl. But you'll be as dead as that old critter on the porch by then!'

As the sudden realization of what the two vicious killers had in store for her sank in, Nancy Davis screamed out at the top of her voice.

The trouble was that there was no one in the ghost town to either hear or help her.

8

Dust drifted up into the starlight off the hoofs of the exhausted horses as their masters viciously continued to spur them on and on. The six outlaws had ridden high and wide of the trail which, they knew, cut its way through the boulders and dense brush far below them. For these men knew that they had to remain unseen until it was time to strike.

Stone knew that if Adams were to have even the slightest suspicion that outlaws were somewhere ahead of him and his cowboys, the wily rancher would never continue on to Devil's Canyon.

The deadly outlaw had led his riders through the uncharted regions far above the established route used by so many others over the years. He had to get as far ahead of Adams and his Bar

10 riders as possible. He had to reach Devil's Canyon where the trail was at its narrowest if he were to execute his plan of bushwhacking them.

Stone had never been a man to square up to anyone if it were possible to back-shoot them instead. Satan himself must have designed the high-walled narrow trail known as Devil's Canyon, for it was the most perfectly natural place to get the drop on an unsuspecting traveller.

Some said that a great river had once carved its way through the solid rock. But if it had been a river, there was no sign of even one drop of the precious water to be found anywhere in between the golden rock-faces now. Temperatures could rise so high there that only sidewinders managed to exist.

After hours of hard riding, something had caused Stone to haul rein and stop his men as they made their way over the rocky terrain through the moonlight.

The line of six horsemen knew they

had ridden well past the place where the the Bar 10 cowboys had made camp. Stone stood in his stirrups and looked down into the eerie mist which rose from the ground all around their high vantage point.

Whatever it was that had persuaded the lethal outlaw leader to stop his mount, one thing was sure, it was nothing to do with Gene Adams.

'What's wrong, Samson?' Talbot asked as he allowed his own horse to walk over the hard rocks until it was level with Stone's lathered mount.

'I heard me something,' Stone replied in his usual rough drawl. 'Sounded like a shot.'

Talbot bit his lower lip.

'Are ya sure? I never heard nothin' exceptin' the clatter of these horses' shoes on the rocks.'

'That's the trouble. I ain't sure,' Stone admitted. 'But I heard something.'

'Where did it come from?' Carson Farmer asked.

Stone shook his head and pointed down toward the ghost town, now shrouded in mist.

'I think it came from down there!'

'Sutter's Corner?' Leroy Chard chipped in.

Stone glanced at Chard.

'Yep. I'd bet me a new hat that a shot was fired down there someplace.'

'I thought that town was deserted.' Farmer rubbed his gloved hand along the neck of his tired horse.

'I heard tell the old hotel is still open for business.' Mooney sighed. 'I could be wrong though.'

Stone stood in his stirrups and twisted around, looking at each of his men in turn.

'Didn't any of you hear a shot? Are ya all deaf?'

There was a collective silence.

Samson Stone dismounted and gave his long reins to Zon Mooney. He dragged his Winchester from beneath his saddle and checked that it was loaded.

'What ya doing, Samson?' Talbot asked. 'We gotta keep going to get to Devil's Canyon before sun-up.'

Stone's eyes burned up through the moonlight at the outlaw's face. He gritted his teeth.

'I'm going down there to take me a look. OK?'

'But we ain't got no time to waste on no wild-goose chases, Samson,' Talbot muttered. 'It's still an awful long ways to Devil's Canyon. We'll be hard pushed to get our horses hid before them Bar 10 critters show up.'

Stone snorted noisily.

'Adams ain't gonna rush to Devil's Canyon. I reckon he'll spend a day or so resting up in that hotel down there. His friend owns it. Nope, I don't figure he'll be in no rush to get to Devil's Canyon.'

'It'd be a damn shame if'n he did and we weren't there waiting for him and them ten thousand dollars in gold he's got stuffed into his bags, Samson,' Chard ventured with a shrug.

'Damn it!' Stone growled as he snatched his reins from Mooney and stepped back into his stirrup. 'I reckon ya right.'

Poke Green watched Stone steady himself in his saddle.

'Why don't we head on down to Sutter's Corner and take us a look, boys? Adams and his cowboys are asleep miles back. We could put Samson's mind at ease.'

Stone thrust his rifle back into its scabbard and gathered his reins up against his chest. He eyed Green.

'The trouble is if we ride down there and that hotel is still open, the folks there will see us. That will alert Adams when he shows up that he ain't alone on the trail.'

'You was gonna go down there on ya own.' Green said.

'I was going to sneak on down there.' Stone nodded. 'There's a difference.'

Suddenly the sound of an ornery mule caught all six men's attention and they dragged their six-shooters from their holsters within seconds of one another. The sound of a half-dozen gun hammers being cocked echoed all about them as a crusty old man appeared over the ridge before them. He walked towards them leading his noisy mule behind him.

The man stopped and squinted into the moonlight.

'It's just an old miner, Samson,' Talbot said. He released his hammer and slid his gun back into his holster. 'There's still a few of the old fools around these parts searching for the mother lode.'

Stone kept his gun trained on the man as he teased his horse forward. The man remained frozen to the spot as his wrinkled eyes watched the approaching rider.

'Who are you?' Stone asked.

The old man looked confused.

'I'm General Lee,' the man giggled. 'Don't ya recognize me, young 'un?'

'Leave him, Samson,' Chard said. 'He's loco. They all end up like that after they've spent so much time up here looking for gold.'

The outlaws pushed their guns back into their holsters and watched as Stone copied their actions.

'Where ya headed, General?' Stone asked, leaning down to the smiling old man.

'I'm gonna go and have me a few drinks.'

'Where?' Stone pressed.

'Down at the hotel. Where else?'

'So it's still open for business?' Stone smiled.

'Sure is. Got some real good sipping-whiskey down there and no mistake.' The old man nodded.

'You like whiskey?'

'Yep!'

Stone curled his finger. The man took a step closer.

Suddenly without warning, Stone thrust a long bladed knife into the old man's chest. The blade was so long that it went right through the helpless figure. Stone repeated the action three more times before the thin figure crumpled in a heap at the hoofs of his mount. The startled mule gave out a pitiful cry and then ran sure-footed down the rocks away from them.

Samson Stone straightened up and wiped the blade of his knife along his pants leg. He then slid it back into the neck of his right boot. He turned his horse and looked at the stunned faces behind him.

'What's wrong, brethren?' He smiled.

'What ya want to do that for, Samson?' Mooney gasped. 'That old critter was no threat to us.'

Stone pulled out his Bible and waved it over the dead body before returning his attention to his riders.

'Are you all fools? That old man confirmed that the hotel is still open! Right? He was going to have himself a few drinks down there. Right again? He'd have told them folks down there about us. Right? Them folks would have told Gene Adams about the six riders headed toward Devil's Canyon. Right?'

'Reckon ya right, Samson.' Talbot nodded as he stared at the body of the old man. The moonlight reflected off the blood-soaked shirt.

'Yeah, you're right, Samson!' Mooney grunted.

'I'm always right coz the sweet Lord makes it so,' Stone raged as he pushed his Bible back into his deep trail-coat pocket. 'Never forget that and you'll all live a tad longer.'

The outlaw leader hauled his reins hard to his right and tapped his spurs. The horse continued on over the rocks with the five riders trailing it. They would continue so until they reached Devil's Canyon.

Once there, they would lie in wait for the four riders.

Samson Stone guided his mount down through the high ragged peaks towards the huge boulders which led to their ultimate destination. With every step of his tall mount, he wondered whether it *had* been a shot that he had heard a few minutes earlier.

If so, who fired it? And at what?

The outlaw hated puzzles.

Or was it just the wild imaginings of a twisted and tired mind starved of sleep for too long?

9

Apache Springs was a small but vital stop which every passing train had to use on its long journey to and from Texas. It consisted of two wooden buildings and a water-tower. One of the buildings was a large barn which held freshly cut wood for the trains' fireboxes and the other structure was part telegraph office and part living-quarters for the four railroad workers.

All four workers had been alerted to the approaching train's imminent arrival by the hooting of its whistle. They stood outside the well-illuminated telegraph office, waiting as they had done count-less times before. Each confident in his own ability to do his job quickly and efficiently.

Even in the darkness they could see the plumes of smoke billowing from the big black chimney long before they actually set eyes upon the train itself. Red-hot cinders rose up into the air amid the smoke.

One of the workers made his way across the steel tracks to the water-tower and started to climb up the wooden ladder to the platform. Another headed to the barn, whilst a third waved a lantern back and forth to signal the train-driver.

The huge locomotive slowed as it neared the water-tower. Steam hissed like a hundred serpents from between its wheels as the huge train rolled to a stop. The engineer and his stoker came out from their cab and started to help the railroad worker haul the huge water-chute away from the tower until its spout was directly over the train's boiler.

None of this hard work was seen by the Bar 10 cowboys, who had yet to test the beds that Gene Adams had secured for them so they might travel home in unaccustomed comfort. The interiors of the two coaches were luxurious by any standards, yet they made the young cowboys inside them uneasy. Most men who had worked as hard as they had since leaving the huge Bar 10 cattle ranch would have accepted the soft beds and already been asleep.

These cowboys were all wide awake. Some played cards whilst others simply remained propped up against well-padded chairs. The two coaches were filled with most of the Bar 10's top cowpunchers. Not one of them had been able to accept that this was something they had earned: a bonus that Adams had been willing to pay for.

They just felt guilty that the man whom they respected above all others was somewhere out there on the trail, sleeping in a bedroll on rock-hard ground. If the train was shunned by the famed rancher, then it followed that they too ought not to be inside its splendid coaches.

The cowboys had accepted the well-cooked meals and free drinks, but that had been hours earlier. Now they were unable or unwilling to use the beds and were bored.

However rough the trail got during a trail drive, there was a unity that all the lean men enjoyed. The simple pleasure of sitting around a roaring camp-fire until it was your turn to ride was all these men knew.

They felt like fish out of water aboard the train.

Rip Calloway sat opposite Happy Summers tossing cards into his upturned Stetson. He glanced around at the other cowboys in his coach and knew that they all felt the same. He noticed that the train was coming to a halt by glancing out of the large window.

'How come we stopped?' Larry Drake asked as he walked into Rip's coach.

Happy Summers pressed his nose up against the window-pane.

'Taking on water, Larry,' he replied.

'Then this must be Apache Springs.' Rip Calloway sighed and tossed his cards down on to the floor.

Happy pulled away from the glass.

'How far do ya figure this train has come since we boarded her?'

'Hard to tell for sure.' Drake bent his knees, shrugged and pointed at the window. 'Not as far as it seems though. We've been on level ground going round the back of those mountains. They go all the way up to them falls near Devil's Canyon. Gene and the boys are headed in a straight line over that hunk of rock.'

Rip rose and stomped his cowboy boot down hard.

'Darn it! I can't keep quiet no longer. This ain't right. Us sitting in here like a bunch of old ladies.'

'You mean us taking the easy way home while Gene and the boys are having to rough it by riding over them rocks and all?' Larry asked.

Rip nodded.

'Yep. I feels darn sick in my craw. Gene and old Tomahawk are too old to be riding out there without us to protect them.'

'They got Johnny and Red with them,' piped up one of the cowboys from the back of the coach.

'Red ain't gonna be no use if'n they run into trouble.' Rip nodded.

'What kind of trouble?' another of the cowboys asked.

Rip stretched himself up to his full height. He was by far the tallest of all the Bar 10 cowboys.

'Gene's got himself a lot of gold in his saddle-bags! That sort of bait can lure a lot of trail trash. He needs us there to protect him.'

Happy stood and rubbed his full stomach.

'We had us some fine vittles earlier, but I'm for getting off this boneshaker and riding after the boys. These beds are just too soft for real men to sleep on.'

'Happy's right!' a voice shouted down the length of the coach.

The rest of the Bar 10 cowboys in the car all stood at the same moment and hooted in agreement.

'So are we gonna stay on this train or are we gonna dismount here?' Rip shouted out. 'I'm for getting our horses off them flatbeds and saddling up. Who's with me?'

'Yeeehar!' the united voices called out.

A train conductor came scurrying into the carriage when he heard the noise of the cheering cowboys.

'What's all this ruckus? Calm down! I don't want no damage done to these coaches.'

Larry Drake leaned close to the small man in the blue peaked cap.

'Tell the driver, we're getting off here. We've had our fill of this soft life.'

The conductor looked shocked.

'But you can't get off here. Adams has paid for the the trip back to Texas.'

Rip glanced down from his full height.

'You gonna tangle with the Bar 10, mister?'

The conductor's eyes flashed around the cowboys' faces as they stared hard at him. He swallowed hard.

'OK! But if you get off here, I can't give you boys any refunds.'

Happy patted his stomach.

'Don't fret none. We've eaten our fill. Ya can keep the pudding.'

'I said refunds, not pudding,' the man snapped as the cowboys all started to drag their gear off the brass overhead rails and file down the middle of the coach. 'Don't ya know what a refund is?'

Happy eyed the conductor and tapped the side of his head.

'I ain't stupid, mister. I know it's one of them fancy desserts. Right?'

'Exactly!' The conductor shook his head in despair, then moved to one side and allowed the cowboys to make their way to the doorway.

The Bar 10 cowboys dropped down from the train and headed back towards the flatbeds.

'What's going on?' one of the Apache Springs railroad workers shouted out from the barn. 'Nobody gets off the train here.'

'We do!' Larry shouted back.

'We're getting our horses off this boneshaker, mister!' Rip Calloway replied as his friends clambered up on to the flatbeds and started to release the pins that secured the sliding doors.

'But why?' the confused man with his arms filled with logs asked. 'Why get off here?'

Rip stood like a tall Texan tree and rested his hand on his gun grip. He glared at the railroad worker.

'We're getting off here coz we got places to go and folks to see, stranger! I'd think twice about trying to stop the Bar 10.'

10

US Marshal Cody Cannon looked far older than his actual years, due to his liking for his moustache. It hung almost covering his mouth in a fashion that had long gone out of style. Yet to him, it was the one thing which set him apart from the rest of the men who roamed the West. A long, black cigar usually jutted defiantly out from the hidden mouth. Its burning tip always pointed at the object of his attention.

There were other things which also set Cannon apart from other men. Including lawmen. For Cannon had a mind that was as keen as a barber's cut-throat razor. He had read every book he could lay his hands upon concerning the art of detection in his forty-eight years of existence.

To him, every crime scene was far more than just a body and a man with a smouldering gun-barrel. To him crime, and especially murder, was a puzzle. Something to solve. An exercise to stretch his mind. Cody Cannon had few equals and no betters when it came to deductive reasoning.

But there were some crimes and criminals which no logical brain could understand or hope to comprehend: those who killed for killing's sake or took pleasure in the torture of others' bodies and souls.

His brain-power had no way of understanding the workings of twisted minds. All he could do was work out what had happened and then try and bring the culprit to justice.

So it had been for the previous five months. He had ridden from county to county, tracking his prey from one atrocity to the next until he rode into the morning sunlight through the streets of the crumbling buildings of Sutter's Corner and on towards the hotel.

Cannon knew that something was

very wrong as soon as he had spotted the hotel a few hundred yards ahead of him. The sun had been up for nearly an hour, but the lanterns were still lit on the porch.

He had guided his tall black stallion with his left hand whilst holding on to his cocked and readied Colt as he approached the hotel.

The lawman knew that coal-oil was far too expensive for anyone to waste it by forgetting to extinguish the flames of their porch lights after dawn.

His fears were confirmed when he saw the dried bloodstained wall and the lifeless body.

Cody Cannon had followed the trail of the two horses from one bloody scene of carnage to another until he wondered whether he would ever get close enough to the Swift brothers to stop them.

Ethan and Clem Swift had no known Wanted posters on them, although they deserved to be branded 'dead or alive'. The brothers had simply killed and robbed at every opportunity ever since they had crawled out from under some rock far to the east.

Their deadly crimes made no sense to the law officers who had tried to investigate them. Without motives there was little to go on. There seemed no way of discovering who the killers actually were. So the culprits had ridden on and on until their lethal handiwork had come to the attention of Marshal Cody Cannon.

Cannon knew that some men did not need a reason to steal, maim or kill. Some men did it simply because they actually could do it.

There was no other reason.

Marshal Cannon had gathered together every scrap of evidence he could find from the string of deadly crimes until he eventually managed to work out the identities of the brothers. Cannon had discovered that the Swift brothers had been in every one of the places where the atrocities had occurred. Cannon had carefully triple-checked every date until he was certain he had worked out their identities.

Months of painstaking investigation had given him names, but what he really needed was the men themselves. There was only one way to achieve that goal.

The hard way.

Cannon had saddled his stallion and started out on the journey which would have defeated any ordinary man. Yet Cody Cannon was far from being an ordinary man. He was someone who would never quit once he had the scent of his prey in his nostrils.

His arrival at Sutter's Corner was no accident.

Cannon had been to a dozen other similar scenes over the previous five months. He had learned how to recognize the hoof-tracks of the Swift brothers' mounts as distinct from all others. Now, outside the hotel, as he dragged his reins up to his sturdy chest, he saw them again.

They had led him here and he knew that the unsuspecting horsemen had no idea that he was, at long last, closing the distance between them.

Yet the pitiful body on the hotel porch, which had already started to attract swarms of flies, was proof that he had again arrived too late.

Without a second thought Cannon dismounted from the black stallion. Like its master, it was used to the sickly-sweet aroma of death. It remained perfectly still and did not shy away from the horrific stench.

Cannon moved over the soft ground, being careful not to disturb any hoof- or footmarks until he had given them his full attention. He nodded to himself as his keen eyes stared down at the familiar horse-shoe imprints.

This was the work of the Swift brothers, he concluded.

Cannon stepped up on the porch and looked down at the body lying in the circle of dried gore.

The marshal reached into his pocket and pulled out a silver case. He extracted a long black cigar and pushed it through his moustache into his mouth. He struck a match and inhaled the strong smoke. He puffed several times to exchange the smell of death for that of the pungent tobacco smoke. Only then did he step closer to the body.

His trained mind studied the area.

Within a few moments the lawman had deduced the chain of events which had preceded and followed the killing of this aged man.

Cannon leaned over and lifted the frozen hand and arm. There was still some flexibility in it. Cannon released it. He knew that whoever this dead man had once been, he had not been dead for more than four hours.

'At last I'm gaining on you!' Cannon muttered under his breath. The marshal had reduced the distance between the killers and himself to a mere dozen or so miles. Even less if they had made camp after their latest killing.

He dropped back down to the soft ground.

There was more evidence here, he thought. Evidence of another victim. Yet this victim was nowhere to be seen. Cannon had spotted the small bloody shoe-marks on the porch. The prints of a female. The dried grass which grew along the entire length of the hotel front was crushed. This was where she had landed, he thought.

Cody Cannon knelt and stared at the ground.

It told him a story that few other people would have been able to interpret. He rose to his feet and removed the cigar from his mouth. A terrible thought overwhelmed the lawman.

Where was she?

They had to have taken her with them!

He placed the cigar back between his teeth and shook his head at the ugly images which filled his thoughts. Perhaps the dead old man was better off than the female, he thought. Cannon had seen what these two men could do to women. What was left after the Swift brothers had finished with them could turn the guts of even the most hardened of souls.

Then he heard the sound of horsemen.

A thousand thoughts filled the lawman's mind.

The marshal rose and turned to face the unseen riders. Both his guns had found his hands. His thumbs hauled back on the hammers as Cannon's eyes narrowed. He held the Colts at hip-level and waited.

A bead of sweat trailed down his temple from his hatband.

11

Marshal Cody Cannon watched the four horsemen cutting their way down from the trail toward Sutter's Corner. His fingers stroked the triggers of his primed weapons as he instinctively trained the barrels on the approaching riders. Dust plumed up off the hoofs.

'Keep coming, I'm ready for you!' Cannon muttered.

For a few seemingly endless moments the lawman just stood and watched as the clouds of dust swirled around the four horsemen. A less courageous man might have squeezed his triggers, but the lawman stood firm and waited.

For unlike the men he hunted, Cannon valued even the lives of his enemies. He would not fire his guns unless they fired on him first or if there was no other opinion.

Cody Cannon took a step forward

and focused hard on the riders. It was obvious that they were not the men he had hunted for nearly half a year.

There were too many of them.

Yet whoever they were, the blinding dust and bright sun shielded their identities from his prying eyes. He stood firm and defied his own fears and kept his deadly guns aimed straight at them.

The horses reached level ground and their masters cleared the choking dust. Cannon now knew that they could see him just as he could see them. Yet they continued to approach.

Suddenly, Cannon recognized them.

The stout lawman heaved a sigh of relief when he spotted the familiar tall chestnut mare and pinto pony of the lead riders. It had been about a year since he had last encountered the famed Gene Adams and his trusty pals. Adams was not a man whom it was easy to forget.

Cannon released the hammers of his weapons, slid them back into their holsters and nodded to the rancher.

Adams raised his left hand and stopped his mare a dozen feet from the marshal. He looped his reins around his saddle horn and rubbed his face with his gloved fingers.

'Is that you, Marshal Cannon?' he asked.

'Yep!' Cannon replied. 'It's me, Adams.'

'You staying at the hotel too?' Adams asked. He dismounted and walked towards the stern-faced man. 'Me and the boys thought we'd have a nice sleep in some comfortable beds before we head on back to the Bar 10.'

'Nope. I'm not staying here. I only just got here myself, Adams,' Cannon said. He watched the rancher's three companions getting off their mounts behind the tall Texan.

Adams stopped a few feet from the law officer.

'What's wrong, man? You look like you seen a ghost.'

Cody Cannon turned his head until

it was aimed at the hotel porch. Gene Adams looked to where the marshal was aiming the gaze of his hooded eyes. He swallowed hard at the gruesome sight.

'I've been trailing two killers. Their trail led here. I got here a few hours late.'

'Dear Lord!' Adams gasped in stunned horror.

'What's wrong, Gene?' Tomahawk asked as he led Johnny and Red towards the two men.

The Bar 10 rancher did not reply. He simply removed his ten-gallon hat, held it across his chest and slowly paced across the dusty ground towards the porch.

'Oh no!' Johnny Puma stopped in his tracks and stared at the body. 'Is that Old Man Davis?'

Cannon sighed.

'I don't know who it is, son,' he admitted. 'All I know is that he's dead. Shot at close range by a rifle.'

Tomahawk squinted at the marshal.

'How canya tell it was a rifle, Marshal?'

'The bullet hole, Tomahawk. A .45 or a .44 would have left a hole big enough to ride a horse through at the range the killer opened up from,' Cannon explained. 'Nope. It had to be a rifle.'

Johnny rushed to Adams's side and grabbed his left arm.

'Is it Davis, Gene?'

Adams looked down at the troubled youngster.

'Yep. It's him OK, Johnny.'

'What about Nancy?' There was panic in the cowboy's voice. Adams turned and looked at the marshal.

'Any sign of the girl, Cannon?'

Cody Cannon strode across to the rancher with Tomahawk and Red on his heels. He pointed at the bloody footprints that covered the porch.

'She was here. Look at the marks of her shoes. There was a struggle and she was dragged off the porch about there. As far as I can determine she must have been taken by the men I'm chasing. We have got to find her fast before she suffers.'

Adams turned away from the body.

'Who are the men you're chasing, Cannon?'

'Brothers,' Cannon answered. 'Ethan and Clem Swift.'

'I ain't heard of them.' Tomahawk sniffed.

'Few folks have.' The marshal sighed. 'What's the name of the girl? How old is she?'

'Her name's Nancy, Marshal. Nancy Davis.' Johnny went pale and drifted away from the four other men as he tried to calm himself. 'She's a couple of years younger than me.'

Adams looked at Tomahawk and nodded.

The old-timer returned the nod and clambered up on to the porch. He disappeared into the hotel for a few moments, then returned into the morning sunlight. He dropped down to the dusty ground, then walked all around the men who were staring at the marks left by the Swift brothers.

Cannon edged closer to Adams.

'I take it Tomahawk knows a little about tracking?'

'Tomahawk's the best there is, Cannon,' Adams whispered.

'I'm pretty good at it myself,' Cannon added.

'Maybe so, but you ain't as good as him.' Adams sighed. 'He can find tracks on solid rock.'

Tomahawk scratched his beard. 'Don't that beat all.'

'What, old-timer?' Gene Adams asked.

'They headed off in the direction of the falls.' Tomahawk was confused. 'That don't make no sense at all. The trail to Devil's Canyon is an easier route south. Why would they choose to ride up into them trees? That's a dead-end trail.'

Cannon glanced at Adams.

'I'm thinking that they might be headed up there to have their fun with that poor girl. Once she's served her purpose, they'll do to her what they did to this old man. Then they'll leave her body up there for the bears to feed on.'

'But why would they ride into a dead end?' Red asked.

'Maybe they don't know that it is!' Tomahawk said.

'Just like they don't know that I've been on their trail for the last five months.' Cannon nodded. 'Those killers think that they've gotten away with all the murders they've left in their wake, boys. That might just work to our advantage.'

Johnny pushed Red aside and squared up to the marshal.

'You sayin' that they'll kill Nancy?' he shouted.

Cannon nodded silently.

Adams stepped between the two men and wrapped his arm around the youngster's shoulder. He inhaled hard, then spoke firmly into the trembling cowboy's ear.

'Easy, son! You losing your head ain't gonna help Nancy none, is it. We have to stay calm. This ain't Cody Cannon's fault. We're damn lucky he's here. He knows a lot more about these killers than we do. That can help us get the drop on the critters. Right?'

Johnny nodded quickly.

'Right!'

Adams turned to Cannon.

'We have to catch them *fast*!'

'Yep. Real fast,' the lawman agreed. 'I know the men but I don't know the lie of this land around here. What falls does Tomahawk mean, Adams?'

Gene Adams stepped out into the blazing sun. His tanned features were like granite and his white hair moved in the gentle breeze. He raised a gloved hand and pointed.

'There's a big river up there past the trees. It drops down suddenly into a lake. They're up there, Cannon.'

'Can they get away from us?'

Adams shook his head.

'Nope. There's only one way up or down that hill from here, Cannon. Ain't nobody ever been able to cross that river and live to tell the tale. The current's too strong. Anything that steps in that water gets swept off the top of the falls.'

Tomahawk pulled out the deadly hatchet after which he was named and ran his thumbnail across its honed blade.

'We got them trapped like rats in a barrel!'

'Even rats can be dangerous when they're cornered, old friend,' Adams said.

Red Hawke walked up to Adams.

'Are we gonna bury this man, boss?' he innocently asked the tall Texan.

Adams reluctantly shook his head and faced the others.

'We ain't got enough time, Red. We have to ride now if'n we're going to catch up with the scum who've got Nancy. We'll bury Davis when we return here.'

'He's gonna be mighty ripe by then, boss.' Red shrugged.

'It can't be helped, son.' Adams

replaced his black hat on his head and tightened its drawstring. 'Get yourself on your horse.'

Red walked to his horse.

Johnny grabbed the mane of his pinto and threw himself up on to his saddle. He steadied himself.

'I'm ready!'

Tomahawk mounted his gelding.

'You boys follow me. I'll find 'em!'

Cannon stepped into his stirrup and pulled himself up on top of his black stallion. He said nothing as he turned the horse around to face the Bar 10 men.

Gene Adams placed his left hand on his saddle horn and hoisted himself up on top of his chestnut mare. He tapped his spurs.

'Come on, Amy!' he said to his horse. 'We got us a little girl to find and help.'

12

The two riders, with their captive, reached the top of the tree-covered hillside before stopping their exhausted mounts. They were strangers in this landscape and had thought that they could continue their long ride south once their horses cleared the high ground. But they should have heeded the warnings which had grown louder and louder the higher their horses got to the hill's summit.

The waterfall could not be seen, but it could be heard. Its sound was deafening, like a locomotive under full throttle.

The Swift brothers had wondered what could be making such a deafening din. Neither rider had ever encountered anything so defiantly powerful before. They had reached the water's edge and stared at the wide river as sunlight danced across its turbulent surface in front of them. There were trees across on the other side of the river, just like the ones they had navigated between for the previous three hours to reach this spot. Yet they knew there was no way that they would ever get close to them. The opposite riverbank was only a matter of a hundred feet away. It might as well have been a mile. The water raged past the noses of their drinking mounts as Ethan Swift slid off his saddle and held on firmly to his reins.

'We ain't gonna get to Texas this way, Clem.'

Clem looked left and right.

'It is kinda rough, ain't it.'

Ethan glanced at his brother, still mounted with the handsome female perched in front of him astride the saddle horn. They had gagged her beautiful mouth and tied her thin wrists, but her eyes still burned like a raging thunderstorm. If looks could kill, the Swift boys would have been six feet under hours earlier.

'You gonna let that girl drop to the ground, Clem?' Ethan asked as he stepped closer.

Nancy kicked out with her small feet and caught the older brother square on his jaw. He staggered backwards, then rubbed the corner of his mouth. He looked at the blood on his fingers and then laughed.

'She's a real wildcat, Clem. I like them frisky!'

'Remember, she's mine, Ethan!' Clem said, holding on to her waist as tightly as he could. 'You promised me that I got first bite of this apple!'

Ethan nodded.

'OK! OK! I don't give a damn. You have your fun with her and I'll take whatever's left!'

'Promise?' Clem stared down at his bleeding sibling. 'Honest Injun?'

'Honest Injun,' Ethan shouted. 'Now let her drop to the ground so we can unsaddle these horses and rustle us up some vittles.'

Clem slid his hands under Nancy's armpits. His fingers lingered and toyed with her well-secured bosom before she threw the back of her head straight into his face. The impact stunned the rider. He quickly lifted her off his saddle horn as blood trailed down from the bridge of his nose. She dropped to the ground heavily, falling at the feet of the still smiling Ethan.

'Ha! She sure knows how to draw blood, Clem!'

Clem lifted his right arm and ran it across his face. He then stared at the red stain on the filthy shirt-sleeve.

'Ya right!' he said. 'She's a wildcat and no mistake!'

'But she sure is pretty though, Clem,' Ethan noted as he touched her long golden hair. 'A man could do a lot worse than this filly and no mistake.'

Nancy tried to kick out again. This time the elder Swift brother was ready. He grabbed her shoulders and turned her away from him. He then drew Nancy close and slid his own hands down over her shapely form.

'Let go!' Clem snapped.

Ethan released his grip and lowered his head.

Clem leapt from his saddle between his brother and the female. He grabbed at Ethan's shirt-collar and pulled him towards him.

'Leave her be!' he shouted.

Ethan nodded and turned to face the river. He rested his hands on his hips and looked at the fast-flowing water. He knew it was wise to change the subject when his brother was all fired up.

'What do ya reckon that noise is, Clem?'

Clem snorted and kicked at the ground. He felt his temper easing up.

'What noise?' he asked.

'That damn noise!' Ethan put a hand to his ear. 'Listen!'

Clem had heard the sound of the water thundering over the rim of the falls for so long that he had become deaf to it. He turned his scrawny neck and looked to their right. His eyes narrowed as he tried to work out what he was actually looking at.

'Thunder?'

'That ain't thunder!' Ethan snapped. 'Ya needs clouds to have thunder. Look at the sky. Blue! Nope, whatever it is, it sure ain't thunder!'

'The sound's coming from over there.' Clem pointed.

Ethan nodded in agreement.

'Yeah, but why? What ya reckon it is? Rivers don't sound like that. Leastways, none that we've ever seen.'

The younger Swift brother pushed Nancy off her feet on to the damp ground and then pulled his rope down from the saddle horn. He used its loop to circle her feet just above the anklebones. He tightened it, then wrapped the rest of the rope around the girth of a tall straight tree.

'Make sure that knot is good and tight, Clem,' Ethan said as he walked up to the distressed female. 'Reckon we ought to leave her gagged for a while. She looks powerful angry.'

Clem made a double knot, then moved back to his horse. He pulled his Winchester out from its scabbard and jerked his head for his brother to follow. Ethan followed.

Both men walked along the soft, moist riverbank towards the sound that they could not comprehend. With every step the noise grew louder. After they had covered a hundred or so yards, they could see what was making all the noise. They were standing on the very top of the waterfall. Neither brother had ever seen anything like it before. They were amazed and more than a little afraid.

The river was almost all white foam at the edge of the cliff as violent torrents of water surged over the edge of the hidden rocks and fell down the sheer drop into a vapour-veiled lake far below them.

They stood on the wet rocks and gazed in awe at the sight that chilled them both. Far beyond the lake a lot of dense brush and well-nourished trees acted like a wall. Beyond that lay an arid white desert of sand.

'I'll be damned!' Ethan gasped.

'A waterfall!' Clem added.

'We're on top of a waterfall!'

'I don't like it!' Clem moved away from the sheer drop and hugged his rifle. 'A man could get real busted up if he fell down there.'

Ethan moved to Clem's side. They both headed away from the chilling natural wonder and back towards their horses and the hogtied Nancy Davis. For a while Ethan was quiet. He kept walking and looking at the raging river. Every few strides he would glance over his shoulder.

'What ya thinking about, Ethan?' Clem eventually asked as they neared their mounts.

Ethan bit his lower lip and then rested his arms on the saddle of his horse. His eyes never stopped moving. They looked at the water and then at the female. Then they looked at the trees which went far off into the distance, and the mountains beyond.

'I just figured something out.'

'What, Ethan?'

'There ain't no place for us to go except back the way we come,' Ethan said bluntly. 'We're cornered up here.'

Clem returned the rifle to its leather scabbard. He then looked at the scenery that surrounded them before he raised his fender and hooked its stirrup over the saddle horn. He began to unbuckle his cinch straps.

Then his face went blank.

'I'm damned if'n ya ain't right. There ain't no place to go at all, is there.'

'No place 'cept back!' Ethan shrugged and then walked to a tree-stump. He sat down and brooded. The sound of the water thundering over the falls was starting to make his head ache. He glanced into the eyes of the female and then at his younger brother. 'Yep, ya right. We'll have to ride back down to that ghost town if we want to get to Texas, Clem.'

Clem hauled the hefty weight off the

horse's back and dropped it near the female. He then sat down next to Nancy. He stared at her the way a hound looks at a bone with meat on it.

'We ain't in no rush though.'

'Right. There ain't no hurry at all,' Ethan agreed. 'We got us saddle-bags full of fine vittles from that hotel and a bottle of good whiskey. We could probably stay up here for a week or more.'

Clem smiled broadly.

'Reckon she'd last a whole week?'

'Depends on how nice she is to us,' Ethan replied. He watched his brother's fingers stroke their victim's face. 'I'm for killing her if she don't start getting friendly. Females ain't got no worth if they don't act nice to a man.'

Furiously, Nancy kicked out and struggled vainly against her bonds.

'She might get herself shot before sundown!' Clem shrugged and then slapped her face.

This time it was Nancy Davis who bled.

13

The ancient cowboy had lost none of his tracking skills. Tomahawk led the four other riders up the steep trail between the tall trees. Even when the hoof-tracks had deviated from the known trail, the wily Tomahawk had not lost contact with them. The afternoon sun filtered through the high canopies far above them giving a strange half-light to the hillside. Yet none of the horsemen noticed anything apart from the skinny rider who led them.

A thousand war drums could not have sounded more ominous than did the chilling noise created by the distant falls as endless gallons of water continued to flow over its high precipice.

But the Bar 10 riders did not fear this landscape. They had ridden far worse trails in their time. They had only one concern and that was to reach Nancy Davis before her ruthless captors destroyed her too.

It took every ounce of the Bar 10 ranchers' horsemanship for Adams to keep his chestnut mare in close contact with his friend's small quarter horse. This was rugged terrain which mules would have had difficulty in negotiating.

This terrain had misled countless riders over the years into thinking that they had discovered a well-shaded route south towards the Texan border; a trail that allowed them to keep out of the blistering sun which baked everything dry beyond Devil's Canyon and the merciless desert.

But all five riders knew that this trail led nowhere except to the banks of an unnamed river which was impossible to cross even during the summer months.

Tomahawk hung over the neck of his gelded black mount and urged the trusty young horse on. His ancient eyes had long lost their ability to see anything at distance but they could still spot the tracks of anything he chose to hunt.

The horses wound their way up the hillside for nearly an hour before the old-timer eased back on his reins and waved his four followers to a halt.

All the horsemen stopped in single file behind the bony man in the weathered buckskins. They held their mounts in check as he threw his leg over his horse's neck and dropped silently to the ground.

Adams dismounted.

'What's wrong, Tomahawk?'

Tomahawk shook his head and then squinted up through the brush which loomed like a pack of green monsters over them.

'I reckon we'd be better off heading up there, Gene!'

Adams turned his head.

'Through the brush? You want us to leave the trail?'

'Not all of us, Gene,' Tomahawk corrected. 'We should split up into two groups. Some stay on the trail and keep going, and a couple of others climb straight up towards the top of the hill.'

Adams glanced at Cody Cannon who had just eased himself off his black stallion and was heading towards them.

'Tomahawk figures we'd be better off splitting up, Cannon.'

The thoughtful marshal nodded.

'He might just be right, Adams. The Swift boys have no reason to suspect that there's anyone on their trail, but whoever rides up to the top of this hill is going to draw their gunfire. If a couple of us cut up through the trees on foot, we might get lucky and catch them unawares.'

Adams raised an eyebrow.

'You reckon?'

'Yep. I do.' Cannon rested his hands on his gun grips and looked up at the severe wall of trees and brush that towered over them. 'Two men might just be able to get the drop on those two evil Swift boys if they take the tough route up there.'

'The riders have to wait until the men on foot have reached the high ground though,' Adams said. 'We need to get them kidnappers confused.'

'Yep!' Cannon agreed.

'The riders will be taking the biggest risk!' Adams said. 'It's hard to keep horses quiet at the best of times. They'll draw fire like bees to pollen.'

The lawman nodded.

'I know but we have to risk it.'

The rancher leaned over the marshal.

'Am I getting your drift? Are you saying that it's you and me going to do the climbing, Cannon?'

'Yep.'

The Bar 10 rancher inhaled deeply and gave the idea some thought. It had been a long while since he had climbed anything except the height of his horse until he reached its saddle. He wondered if he still had the wind in his lungs and strength in his long legs actually to get to the top of this hill.

'How far do you reckon it is to the top?'

'A quarter-mile or so,' Cody Cannon guessed. 'Twice as far for me with these short stumpy legs of mine.'

'OK.' Adams smiled.

Johnny Puma moved to the two men. 'I'm comin' with you, Gene. OK?'

Gene Adams could see the fire in the youngster's eyes. He wanted to kill the Swift brothers and that was not too far from his own feelings, but sometimes Johnny could lose control. For a decade or more, Adams had groomed him and managed to stop the young cowboy from returning to his old ways. He knew that Johnny had once been an outlaw until he had sought and found refuge on the Bar 10. Adams realized that it was far safer for all concerned to have the cowboy close, if he were ever going to be able to keep him under control.

'Good idea, Johnny,' Adams said, patting his back. 'I reckon we might need that gun-speed of yours.'

'And accuracy!' Johnny added.

'Are you any good with those Colts,

Johnny?' Cannon asked.

Gene Adams interrupted.

'There ain't nobody better, Cannon.'

'I just hope we're in time.' The marshal sighed heavily.

'You and Red keep riding up the trail, Tomahawk,' Adams ordered. 'When you reach the top, try not to break cover too fast. Make a lot of noise. Understand?'

'Ya darn tootin' I understands, Gene.' Tomahawk nodded as he watched the three men tying their reins to tree-branches.

'Be careful, you old fossil!' Johnny said.

Tomahawk crooked a finger at Red who spurred his horse and rode past the other men and their mounts until he reached the side of the old-timer.

'What ya want, Tomahawk?' Red drawled slowly. 'How come we stopped?'

'Never mind that. Now, listen up, Red boy,' Tomahawk whispered. 'You and me got the tough job here. We have to ride up the trail 'til we reaches the top of this hill. Right?'

'Right.' Red nodded.

'We gotta draw the fire of them cowards up there so that Gene, Johnny and Cannon can get the drop on 'em. OK?'

Red watched as Gene Adams led Cannon and Johnny up between the trees and into the dense brush. He then looked down at Tomahawk again.

'Is somebody gonna shoot at us?'

Tomahawk mounted his gelding and gathered up his reins. He raised his bushy eyebrows and tapped his feet against the side of the horse.

'I reckon so. It's a good bet anyways.'

'What'll I do when they start shootin' at us, Tomahawk?'

'C'mon, Red boy. I'll tell ya when to duck!'

The amiable young cowhand trusted the old man like all kind-hearted souls trust their elders. He slapped the long lengths of his reins and followed the wily Tomahawk along the twisting trail that led up to the top of the tree-covered hill. The further they rode, the louder the noise of the unseen waterfall became.

★ ★ ★

Samson Stone and his five henchmen had made good progress through the long night and reached Devil's Canyon a good hour before dawn. They had hidden their six mounts to the south of the canyon and then made their way a couple of hundred yards into the narrow high-sided trail. Stone had hand-picked the massive rocks for each of his men to hide behind before he himself took cover.

At first the six men had been bathed in the shade of the high sand-coloured rocks which loomed over them like giants. Then the merciless rays of the sun found them. There was no hiding-place from the deadly, blinding orb as it climbed higher and higher into the blue, cloudless sky.

The rest of the outlaws started silently to question the wisdom of their leader. For all they knew Gene Adams and his three travelling companions would spend days at the hotel at Sutter's Corner.

Would they be forced to remain in the lethal Devil's Canyon both day and night? To freeze during the hours of darkness and bake during the day?

Samson Stone and his men had already started to suffer. No amount of canteen water could quench their thirst or prevent their skin from peeling off their faces and hands. They had already started to burn as they discovered to their cost why this place had such a colourful name.

Yet none of Stone's men dared venture away from the hiding-places that he had chosen for them. His venomous wrath was even more fearsome than the deadly sun above their sweat-soaked heads.

The outlaws would wait until Adams and his Bar 10 cowboys showed up with the saddle-bags of golden coins or Samson Stone changed his mind and permitted them to leave their lethal hiding-places amid the white-hot rocks.

Hour after hour saw their canteens get drier.

Just like the outlaws themselves.

14

The Swift brothers had eaten more than half of the provisions they had stolen from the hotel far below at Sutter's Corner. They had also drunk nearly all of the bottle of whiskey that they had also removed from the hotel bar. Yet neither man was drunk or full. There was something else burning at their craws. Something still undone.

They stared at the flickering flames of their small fire and the blackened coffee-pot which stood in the ashes. The sun was almost directly above the small clearing near the raging river. It was hotter than the bowels of hell and the two men had already started to sweat like men sweat when they have a female close at hand.

A female whom they both wanted.

Clem had remained closer to the helpless female than his brother since they had arrived at the river. Yet her gagged mouth had not stopped her fiery eyes from keeping his wayward hands at bay. The younger of the Swift siblings was actually afraid of Nancy Davis. She was bound hand and foot and yet he was still afraid of her.

But Ethan was not as slow or bashful as his brother. He had started to move closer to their beautiful prize and now was within mere inches of taking her. Ethan reached over her and teased at her button-fronted dress.

Clem glanced around at his brother.

'You keep ya damn hands off her, Ethan!' he growled in a low telling tone. 'She's mine. I told ya before, she's mine. You just back off!'

'Then why don't ya have her?' Ethan shouted back. 'I've been waiting for hours for you to do something, but ya just sitting there like an old gelding.'

Nancy Davis lay between them. Her eyes darted from one brother to the next as she continued to struggle to break free of her bonds.

Clem gritted his teeth.

'I ain't ready yet!'

'Then let me . . . '

Clem rose to his feet and looked down at Ethan. There was a fury in his face that few men had lived to tell of. He was breathing hard and clenched both fists.

'I'll kill ya if ya make a move on her! Ya know that I ain't joshing, Ethan!'

Ethan eased himself up until he was standing eye to eye with his brooding brother. Many men had looked into the ruthless eyes of Clem Swift a fraction of a second before they had died. Yet Ethan had no fear of him.

He knew Clem too well.

'Are you waiting for sundown?' the elder Swift taunted. 'Ya scared of doing something in the light of day? Worried I might laugh?'

Clem spat.

'Ya trying to be funny?'

'Damn right, Clem! What ya gonna do about it 7' Ethan nodded slowly as spittle dripped off his unshaven face.

He leaned over and held on to the top of the girl's blood-stained dress. He jerked at the fabric and tore it. Ethan Swift then smiled at the exposed flesh. He had never set eyes on anything that tempting before. 'Look at her, Clem. Damned if she ain't got the whitest skin I ever done seen. A man could die happy if'n he's had her under him.'

'I'm gonna kill ya! That's what I'm gonna do! I'm gonna kill ya!' Clem screamed.

He leapt over Nancy and grabbed Ethan's throat. His fingers squeezed with every ounce of his brutal strength. Both men fell backwards and hit the ground hard.

'Let go of me, ya crazy fool!'

The words faded as once again Clem's hands started to choke the life out of Ethan. They scrambled feverishly over the ground and then over Nancy. Both men head-butted one another like mountain goats. Blood trickled down Clem's face from a two-inch gash above his left eye.

Ethan pushed both his hands up between his brother's arms until his own fingers found Clem's eyes. His long dirty fingernails clawed at the skin. More blood flowed down the face of the younger Swift brother. Clem brought up his right knee as hard as he could. A pained expression etched Ethan's features. They rolled over and over until they reached the muddy water's edge. Fists flew and both men fell into the ice-cold river.

It was a sudden and sobering shock.

Only then did they release their holds on one another. As the strong current dragged Ethan off his feet, Clem grabbed hold of him and hauled his sodden sibling out of the water.

He dropped him. Ethan's face hit the mud.

Suddenly, Clem noticed their unsaddled mounts turning their heads away from the river. Both had their ears aimed at the trees a hundred feet away.

Clem dropped down beside his brother.

'You young pup! I ought to kill ya good!' Ethan spluttered as lumps of mud fell from his mouth and landed beside his brother.

'We got company, Ethan!' Clem said, pulling his Colt from its holster and cocking its hammer. Water dripped from the weapon as both brothers looked at each other.

'Who?' Ethan asked. 'Where?'

'Whoever they are, they're over yonder.' Clem pointed a finger to where they knew the trail opened up just beyond the clearing. 'I can see me two riders in the shadows. Can you see them?'

'I see them!'

'Who do ya reckon they are?'

'Whoever they are, they'll be dead folks pretty soon, Clem!' Ethan wiped his mouth and reached down along his prostrate body to his gunbelt. He hauled his gun out and yanked its hammer with his thumb.

Clem aimed his gun and squeezed its trigger. The hammer fell but the gun did not respond.

'That river has put paid to my gun, Ethan.'

Ethan tried to fire his own gun but it too failed to work.

'Mine's wet as well!'

Clem holstered his Colt. Ethan crawled closer to his brother and nudged him. Both men stared over Nancy's helpless form to where their horses seemed to be staring.

'We gotta get our rifles!'

Clem shifted his gaze to their saddles and tack next to Nancy and the smoking fire. Their rifles were in their scabbards next to the struggling female.

'C'mon! We get the rifles and we do us some shootin'!'

They started to crawl away from the water's edge. Both stayed low on their bellies and slithered across the churned-up muddy ground like a pair of sidewinders. They moved between the long legs of their horses, using every blade of tall grass as cover on their way back to their saddles beside the camp-fire. Nancy Davis was between them and the two riders they had spotted.

Like the vermin in human form that they were, they were using Nancy as a shield.

Clem reached his rifle first. He dragged the long Winchester out of its leather scabbard and cranked its mechanism just as his brother placed a hand on the wooden stock of his own carbine.

'We gonna open up on them from here?' Ethan asked as he pushed the lever of his seldom-used rifle down and heard a bullet engage inside its magazine. 'They're a mighty long ways off from us, Clem.'

'I can see them.' Clem smiled. 'And what I can see, I can shoot.'

Ethan knew his brother was right. He had never seen anyone outshoot his brother with any type of rifle.

Clem licked his thumb and stroked it across the sights. He pulled up the rifle until he was staring down its length.

'Reckon this'll be a turkey-shoot. We got us two easy targets and they got nothing to aim at. The saddles and the girl will give us cover. Right?'

'Right!' Ethan smiled slowly.

15

The canopy of tree branches ended just before the wide expanse of tall grass which led to the powerful river. Tomahawk steadied his horse and vainly squinted out into the clearing from the shadows of the dense woodland. The blazing sun made it difficult for young eyes to see and almost impossible for old ones. At last the ancient cowpoke turned and looked at Red for help. The gangling youngster was sitting high in his saddle a few feet away from him. Tomahawk rotated his tongue around his toothless mouth and tried to whistle.

'You spittin' at me, Tomahawk?' Red asked slowly.

'Pay attention, Red boy,' the old-timer said, leaning across the distance between them. 'Can ya see anything? Them killers or the gal? Use them young eyes of yours.'

'I'll try, Tomahawk.' Red eased his mount forward. 'It's kinda bright out there though.'

Plumes of gunsmoke rose from the rifles of the pair of Winchesters in the Swift brothers' arms. Then the deafening confirmation filled the ears of the two Bar 10 men.

Suddenly the leaves were torn off the low-hanging branches of the trees which surrounded them by the bullets as they cut through the hot air. The sound of rifle fire echoed around the clearing.

Tomahawk threw himself off his saddle and down on to the ground. He turned and shouted at Red.

'Get off ya horse, boy! They seen us!'

The long-legged young cowboy felt his mount rear up beneath him. He tried to hang on but it was impossible. Another volley of shots rang out. His mount made a pitiful noise as its flesh was hit by the rifle bullets. Red fell backwards over his saddle cantle and bedroll. He landed in the brush and then watched his horse crash down beside him.

'They shot my horse, Tomahawk!' Red gasped. 'Them critters shot my horse!'

'Get ya head down or they'll shoot that as well,' said the wily old man. His right hand drew the deadly Indian hatchet from his belt.

Red crawled to the old man's side.

'You said ya was gonna say 'duck', Tomahawk!'

'I did!' Tomahawk lied. 'Ya just a tad deaf.'

'I sure liked that horse,' Red drawled.

Tomahawk gripped his axe firmly in his right hand. 'Can ya see them?'

More shots rang out. One hit the crown of Red's Stetson and tore it off his head. He raised a shaking hand and pointed.

'There they are.'

'How far away?'

'Two hundred feet or so. Why?' Red asked innocently.

Tomahawk put the hatchet under the nose of the startled cowboy.

'I'm just trying to figure if I can hit them with this old toothpick from this distance, ya young whipper-snapper.'

Red shook his head.

'There's a lady tied up right in front of them and their saddles, Tomahawk. Reckon ya might hit her rather than them if'n ya throws that thing.'

Tomahawk squinted again.

'Is you sure, boy?'

'Yep.' Red nodded. 'She's got real pretty yellow hair.'

'That's Nancy. Don't that take the biscuit? The yellow varmints are using her to hide behind.' Tomahwk scratched his beard. 'The cowards!'

Red gripped the arm of the older man.

'I see Gene and the marshal and Johnny over yonder. They just made it up that old hill of trees.'

'About time they showed up!' Tomahawk sniffed. 'Leaving us to hold the fort whilst he picks daisies,

I'll bet ya. Leastways, we got them killers pinned down.'

'I thought we was the ones who was pinned down, Tomahawk.'

'Hush that mouth, Red boy!' The old man wrinkled up his eyes and glared at his companion. 'We've softened 'em up for Gene and the boys!'

More bullets blasted from the rifles and came close. Too close for comfort. Both prostrate cowboys had felt the heat of the deadly lead as it passed a few inches above them.

'What'll we do now?' asked a confused Red. 'They're startin' to get awful close with their bullets.'

Tomahawk could see the vague images of Adams, Cannon and Johnny move out of the clearing behind the Swift brothers. He gave a toothless grin.

'Stay still and wait, Red boy. I reckon the fireworks will start any second now!'

'Huh?'

Tomahawk rolled his eyes.

'Duck!'

Red dropped his head into the grass.

'Stupid young buck!' Tomahawk chuckled.

16

Tomahawk had been right. The fireworks were about to start. More fireworks than a Fourth of July celebration. But these fireworks would explode from the barrels of rifles and guns. They would not seek the heavens, but the flesh of men. They would spit lead and not stop until blood had been spilled.

Clem Swift had been first to spot the three men making their way from the cover of the trees. He swung around on his knees with his Winchester in his hands.

'More of them, Ethan!' he yelled out as he thrust the hand guard of his rifle down and then back up. 'Who in tarnation are they?'

Ethan rolled over and brought his Winchester up to his shoulder. He fired.

'Who knows? Shoot them, Clem! Shoot them!'

Clem fired three shots in quick succession and cursed as he realized that these men were not as easy to hit as most he had encountered. For one thing, these men shot back. A dozen shots sped over the heads of the Swift boys from the guns of Cannon and the Bar 10 cowboys.

Adams dropped down on to his belly in the long grass. The marshal and Johnny copied his action.

'Stay low!' Adams called out. 'They can't hit what they can't see!'

The Swift brothers had a similar theory. They also remained low and hid behind their saddles and the handsome female.

'They dropped down in the grass!' Clem snarled as he cautiously rose up on his knees to try and see where his targets had gone. 'Ya see them? Can ya see them, Ethan?'

Ethan screwed his eyes up until he was focused on the spot where all three had disappeared into the high, swaying grass. 'Shoot low, Clem. Shoot low and ya might just hit one of them!'

Both brothers started to work their repeating rifles hard and sent bullets low into the grass. They had no idea where their enemy was. It was something neither man had experienced before and they did not like it.

For the first time, the hunters were the hunted.

Clem squeezed his trigger and then dropped back down.

'Get my box of cartridges out of my saddle-bags, Ethan.'

Ethan reached over his saddle and dragged the heavy bags over the wide-eyed Nancy. He unbuckled the straps and brought out a cardboard box. It was light. Too light. He shook it before opening it.

'There's only about ten or twelve bullets here, Clem!'

Clem turned and glared into the box. He swallowed hard, then looked up into the face of his brother.

'I thought I had me more than that, Ethan,' he said as he felt his mouth dry of spittle. 'Damn! I thought there was more! Maybe I got me another box! Look!'

Ethan dragged everything out of both satchels of the bags and spread them out between them. There were no more rifle bullets.

'This ain't good,' Ethan muttered. 'We got guns that won't fire and not even enough rifle cartridges to fill one of our Winchesters.'

'You got any rifle bullets?' Clem asked as he loaded his rifle with the bullets.

'You know I hardly ever use my rifle, Clem,' Ethan stated. 'I always borrow some of your bullets. I only got me .45s and they ain't no use in wet six-guns!'

Clem handed two bullets to his brother.

'Slip them into ya Winchester!'

Ethan nodded and did it.

Then they returned their attention to the high, dry grass and the blinding sun which faced them.

Clem blasted another few shots at their unseen attackers before the hand of his sibling grabbed his shoulder.

'What?' Clem snarled.

'Don't waste no more bullets, Clem,' Ethan said. 'We ain't got enough to waste.'

Clem nodded and rested on his knees. He tried to think but it was a habit he had never mastered.

'What'll we do?'

Ethan swallowed hard.

'The girl! We use the girl! She's our ticket out of here!'

Clem's eyes darted towards Ethan's face.

'Ya mean, like a shield?'

'Yep!' Ethan nodded. 'Like a shield! Maybe they're her kinfolk come to get her. They might not want to risk shootin' her if we keep her close.'

'She ain't big enough, Ethan,' Clem said.

Ethan reached across the saddles and dragged Nancy Davis by her blonde

hair over their saddles and then
loosened the rope around her ankles.
He pulled her across him and used his
strong left hand to grip her throat just
below her jaw.

'I got me a feelin' they won't shoot if
we got her between us and their lead!'
he said.

'Are ya sure?' Clem asked.

'Nope!' Ethan replied. 'But we ain't
got no other way of getting out of here.
We're short of bullets and I seen me a
lot of guns between them three critters
over yonder!'

Clem looked at their horses.

'Do ya reckon they'll let us saddle up
if we use her as a shield?'

'There's only one way to find out!'
Ethan abruptly stood and walked away
from their saddles with Nancy across
his front. He kept glancing to his left
and right, knowing that to both sides of
him there were deadly guns.

Clem cocked his rifle again.

'Have ya gone plumb loco, Ethan?'

'Just get ready to shoot anyone that

160

fires at me, Clem!'

Again, the younger Swift brother did exactly as he was told and waited to return fire if Ethan's theory proved to be wrong about their unseen enemies not firing for fear of hitting the girl.

Ethan inhaled and then screamed out in the direction of Adams and his two companions.

'Whoever ya are, ya better not shoot unless ya want to kill this pretty little gal!'

For what seemed an eternity, there was no reply.

17

The young Bar 10 cowboy could not stand it any longer. Johnny Puma jumped up to his full height with both his cocked Colts in his hands. Smoke still trailed from their barrels as he narrowed his eyes and stared hard at the man who held Nancy before him.

'Get ya filthy hands off her, mister!' Johnny shouted at Ethan Swift. 'I'll kill ya if ya don't!'

The laughter could be heard all over the clearing. Clem Swift cautiously raised himself up and stood close to his brother. His fingers moved nervously as he held his Winchester across his chest ready to fire.

Gene Adams stood. He had his golden Colt .45s in his gloved hands. They too were aimed in the direction of the three figures.

162

'Don't shoot, Johnny!' Adams urged. 'Nancy's too close to them varmints. They only got to twitch and you could hit her instead of them.'

Johnny walked closer to the Bar 10 rancher.

'I can hit them both, Gene! I could put a bullet between the eyes of both them before they knew what was happening.'

Adams had seen the deadly accuracy of his young friend's marksmanship many times, but there had never been a situation quite like this one. Never had anyone they knew been so close to their targets.

'No, Johnny!' Adams growled. 'It's too risky!'

Marshal Cody Cannon stood up. He had only one of his guns drawn but it was also aimed at the Swift brothers.

'What do you boys want?' the lawman called out. 'I'm Marshal Cannon and I'm ready to listen to terms!'

Stunned, Gene Adams turned his

head and looked at Cannon in disbelief.

'You ain't thinking of bargaining with them stinking critters are you, Cody?'

Marshal Cannon continued to keep his unblinking eyes on the two men. He knew that at any moment they might open up with their weapons.

'Leave this to me, Adams!' he said out of the corner of his mouth. 'I'm used to dealing with scum. You ain't!'

Few men ever contradicted Gene Adams or had the nerve to give him orders. The tall rancher knew that Cannon had some sort of plan in mind. The trouble was he did not know what that plan entailed.

'What you planning to do, Cannon?' Adams asked. 'I don't want that little girl hurt none. I'll get darn angry if she gets hurt.'

'I hear you, Adams.' The marshal nodded as he kept his hooded eyes aimed on the Swift brothers and their hostage. 'Just keep them guns cocked and let me handle this.'

Reluctantly, Adams agreed.

'OK, Cannon! But if things go wrong — '

'Trust me!' Cannon said.

'We can't do a damn thing, can we.' Johnny cleared his throat. He was desperate to do something to help Nancy. She was special to him and for the first time in his life, he felt helpless. 'We just gotta wait like three old women. You better know what ya doing, Marshal!'

'He does, Johnny!' Adams whispered. 'Cody Cannon knows what he's doing OK.'

'Just have to keep them varmints looking at us, boys,' the marshal said quietly. 'Don't let them look back over their shoulders.'

'What ya mean, Cannon?' Johnny asked.

Cody Cannon continued to stare at the Swifts.

'Tomahawk's moving!' he whispered.

Both Adams and Johnny looked beyond the Swift brothers. The lawman was correct. The wily old-timer had started to make his move silently through the tall grass.

'He'll get himself killed!' Johnny stammered.

'That'll be the day!' Adams rebuked.

'We're gonna saddle our horses and ride out of here!' Ethan shouted at Cannon and his two comrades. 'You try and stop us and we'll kill this girl!'

Cannon shrugged and holstered his gun.

'OK! Get them horses saddled and you can ride out of here. We won't do anything to stop you.'

For some unknown reason Ethan trusted the word of the man with the star pinned to his chest. He looked at his brother.

'Saddle our horses, Clem. We're gettin' out of here!'

'Ya trust that fat old critter?'

'Yep!' Ethan replied. 'He knows I can snap her neck at any time I want. They'll not shoot while I got her by the neck!'

Tomahawk had covered a lot of

ground since the talking had started. He could now see the two men and Nancy clearly as he rolled over on to his side. He brought his deadly tomahawk up to his face and stared at its honed edge. He had killed a lot of people with this trusty old axe during the previous fifty or so years.

But never anyone that had not deserved killing.

Tomahawk looked ahead of him and watched Clem quickly saddling the two skittish horses as Ethan continued to hold Nancy between himself and the three men a hundred yards away.

Slowly, the oldest Bar 10 cowboy rose out of the dry grass and aimed his left hand at his target whilst leaning back with the deadly weapon in his right.

Like a javelin thrower from ancient times, the old man forced his muscles to tighten like a series of coiled springs. He would not release them until he was certain of hitting what he was aiming at.

Clem dropped the fender of the second horse's saddle and plucked his rifle up off the ground. He had never before worked so hard or so quickly. He had saddled both horses in a matter of two minutes.

'The horses are ready, Ethan!'

Ethan moved closer to his own horse and forced Nancy to mount it before he slipped his boot into the stirrup and threw himself up behind her. He drew his water-logged gun and cocked its hammer before pressing its barrel into her temple.

This would be his ultimate bluff.

'If any of you move a muscle, I'll kill her!' Ethan shouted out at Adams and his two companions.

Cannon took a step forward. Now it was his turn to bluff.

'Mighty big talk for a snivelling worm!' he taunted knowing that he dare not allow either man to look behind them.

Clem Swift mounted and kept his Winchester trained on the three men.

'C'mon, Ethan. We gotta ride!' There was an urgency in his voice.

With every ounce of his strength and decades of expertise, Tomahawk unleashed his axe. The Indian hatchet cut through the hot air so quickly it sounded like a swarm of angry hornets.

The sound drew Clem's attention. He tugged his reins hard to his left just in time to see the tomahawk flying straight at him.

It was the last thing he ever saw.

The curved metal axe-head hit the younger Swift brother in the centre of his face. It did not stop until it had embedded in the rider's brain.

The sheer force of the brutal weapon knocked the lifeless body off its saddle. It landed at the hoofs of Ethan's horse causing it to buck like a mustang. The frightened creature continued to jump up and down until there was little remaining of the younger Swift that was recognizable.

Ethan steadied his mount at last and stared down in disbelief at what was left of Clem. He then saw the old-timer standing defiantly in the swaying grass.

With little time to think, Ethan holstered his useless weapon and then pushed Nancy off his saddle.

He spurred.

The horse leapt into action and galloped.

Gene Adams and Johnny raised their arms and fired their .45s at almost exactly the same moment. Gunsmoke curled out of their gun barrels.

Ethan Swift took all four bullets in his side and went cartwheeling off his saddle. He landed lifelessly at the feet of Tomahawk.

The old cowboy ambled to the twisted body and looked down on it just as Gene Adams ran up to his side with Cannon a few yards behind him.

'That was good shootin', Gene boy,' Tomahawk said. 'I thought ya was going to let the critter go for a minute.'

'He nearly got away,' Adams admitted. 'Another few yards and he'd have reached the brush. I don't think we could have caught the varmint if he'd reached them trees.'

'That was darn fine accuracy with that axe, Tomahawk.' The marshal sighed. 'I never seen a throw like it in all my days.' Tomahawk smiled.

'Gee, ya think so? I'd have gotten them both twenty years ago!'

Gene Adams turned away from the body. He felt no satisfaction in having just killed the ruthless youngster who, with his evil sibling, had killed so many innocent souls.

'You look unhappy, Adams,' Cannon remarked.

'How's a man meant to look when he's just helped kill someone, Cannon?'

'They were vermin!' the lawman added.

'It still don't make me feel any better, Marshal!'

Tomahawk pointed to Red. The cowboy still had his head buried in the grass fifty feet away from where they stood.

'I told him to duck, Gene boy. He

sure is an obedient young critter. Kinda dumb though!'

Adams did not reply. He just stood tall watching Johnny helping the beautiful female back to her feet. She was bruised and battered but still alive. Nancy Davis looked into the Bar 10 cowboy's face then flung her arms around his neck. Their lips met and they kissed.

'Kinda makes ya wish ya was still young, eh Gene?' Tomahawk sighed.

Gene Adams looked at both men and lowered his head.

'Nope. Not really. I'd not want to be their age any longer. I ain't nearly strong enough. Don't you recall that I had my heart busted when I was their age, old-timer? That kinda pain just never goes away, Tomahawk.'

'Reckon not, boy.' The elderly man shrugged.

'What's he mean, Tomahawk?' the lawman asked.

'Best if'n ya don't ask, boy!' came the reply. 'Gene gets kinda upset when folks ask him questions. Times were tough forty years back.'

Marshal Cannon sighed as the Bar 10 rancher walked off towards Red Hawke to tell him he could stand up again. He then saw the pained expression in the rugged, bearded features of the toothless old man.

'I'd better go get my old tomahawk! Makes the blade rust somethin' awful if ya leaves it in dead folks' skulls.'

Cannon nodded to Tomahawk.

He then glanced across at Johnny and Nancy. They were oblivious to everything apart from one another. They were still in each other's arms.

The marshal smiled, turned and walked towards Ethan Swift's confused horse. It still had blood dripping from its saddle.

18

The sun had set long before the riders reached the hotel at Sutter's Corner. Adams and Red had ridden on ahead of the main group to bury what was left of Old Man Davis before his niece arrived back with Johnny, Tomahawk and Cannon. The Swift brothers had served one purpose after their bloody deaths. One of their mounts was used by Red and the other by Nancy to return down the steep hillside.

By the time the four horses caught up with Adams and his youngest cowboy at the hotel perched above the ghost town, there was no sign of what had occurred inside and outside its wooden walls. The entire building smelled fresh after having every drop of blood scrubbed off its weathered boards.

An exhausted Gene Adams sat beneath the porch light, watching the quartet of horses riding towards him. He looked at Red and smiled.

'You did good, Red boy. You'll make the grade one of these days.'

The cowboy grinned. Even his teeth made no sense.

'Shucks, boss. It weren't just me. We both done our best to clean this old place up. Reckon the stink has gone now.'

'Most smells can't stand a good dose of soap and boiling water, son.' Adams nodded. 'Even the smell of death.'

'That Miss Nancy sure is a darn pretty gal, boss.' The awkward cowboy sighed as he stared at the approaching riders.

'Yep,' Adams agreed.

Johnny had ridden beside his old flame for the entire length of the journey down from the top of the tree-covered hills. He slowed his pinto and jumped off its saddle before Nancy had time to ease back on her reins.

Adams watched silently as the cowboy rushed to help the beautiful female down from her saddle. His eyes darted to Red, who was sniffing at the palms of his hands.

'What's the matter, Red?'

'My hands smell kinda girlie,' Red replied. 'Like a woman's.'

'That's the soap, boy! Reckon you ought to use it more often.'

Tomahawk and Cannon stopped their horses and dismounted next to the pinto pony. Both men looked weary from their hard ride as they stood inhaling the scented air.

Adams looked at Red and then pointed at the lathered-up mounts.

'Take them horses to the stable, Red. Unsaddle them and give them plenty of water and grain. Rub them down good coz me and Tomahawk will be heading back to the Bar 10 just after supper.'

'Sure thing, boss.' Red leapt down, took all the reins in his hands and led the exhausted animals towards the hotel's stables.

'We is?' Tomahawk's toothless mouth opened wide. 'We ain't getting to sleep in a nice soft bed tonight?'

Adams smiled. 'I'm afraid not, old-timer.'

Tomahawk made his way up to Adams. He sniffed at the air and then scratched his beard.

'This place sure smells awful pretty, Gene.'

Adams shook his head.

'Don't any of my cowboys recognize the smell of soap?'

'I knows what soap smells like, Gene.' Tomahawk shrugged. 'I just never cottoned to it. I likes natural smells.'

Cody Cannon grinned.

'Like steers and sweat?'

'Sure thing.' The old cowboy nodded. 'Nothin' like the smell of cattle to make the gals take notice.'

Gene Adams could see that even though he and Red had worked hard to remove all traces of the carnage which had occurred here, the horrific images still filled the mind of the young woman. There was a hesitancy in

Nancy as she clung to Johnny and stared at the brightly lit hotel.

'There's some things that no amount of soap can wash away,' Adams whispered to the two men closest to him. Cannon and Tomahawk saw the concern in the face of the rancher.

'Like what, Gene?' Tomahawk asked.

'Memories, old-timer. Bad memories,' Adams replied.

It seemed that no matter how hard the young Johnny tried, he was unable to get Nancy to take even one footstep closer to the large building.

'It's OK, Nancy,' Johnny whispered into her ear. 'There ain't nothing for you to be afraid of.'

Gene Adams stood up, walked across the porch and stepped down on the ground. He moved to the opposite side of the handsome woman, removed his hat and offered his arm.

'May I have the honour of escorting you, Nancy?'

Even in the light of the oil-lanterns, Nancy's beautiful smile was clearly visible. Her eyes flashed as they studied the still handsome face of the silver-haired rancher. She accepted his arm and stepped up on to the porch. Again she paused as the sickening memory of what she had last seen here filled her thoughts. Then she realized that it had been scrubbed clean, leaving no evidence of the brutal murder.

'It's OK, Nancy honey,' Adams said, patting the back of her tiny hand with his gloved one. 'Let's go inside now. We have to prepare supper coz these boys are powerful hungry.'

Nancy Davis took a deep breath then moved forward. She walked into the interior of the hotel clinging to the tall rancher's arm. Every step took courage.

Johnny moved to Marshal Cannon and Tomahawk. He removed his Stetson and scratched his thick head of hair.

'How come she went in there with Gene and not me?'

'Don't get jealous, ya young whippersnapper.' Tomahawk winked.

'Sometimes us older folks can give you young 'uns like Nancy a little extra nerve.'

Cody Cannon smiled.

'Who'd be afraid with Gene Adams at your side, Johnny?'

Johnny beamed.

'That's right!'

'Now go in there and take over from Gene,' Tomahawk instructed his pal. 'Nancy needs ya.'

'Ya right!' Johnny leapt up on to the porch and rushed inside the well-illuminated hotel.

Tomahawk rested down on the edge of the porch and looked down at the ghost town. The marshal stood above him and leaned against the wooden upright.

'Tell me, Marshal,' Tomahawk started, 'how come ya didn't bring the bodies of them Swift boys down with ya? I thought they had bounty on their heads!'

'Nope. Those blood-crazed boys never got themselves arrested for anything,' Cannon told him. 'They weren't worth a penny. I was on their tail for personal reasons. Not financial ones.'

'They hurt someone ya knew?'

Cannon nodded.

'Yep.'

Tomahawk sighed. He knew that Cody Cannon was not the type to go into detail about anything unless he had to do so. The lawman pulled out a cigar from his silver case and placed it between his teeth. He struck a match and inhaled the smoke deeply.

'What you thinking about, old-timer?'

Tomahawk sighed even more heavily.

'I recall when that ghost town was buzzing like a beehive. Folks from every place there is came here to buy and sell and get up to things ya couldn't tell ya mother about. Now look at it. A ruin just like me.'

'Things get old and die,' Cody Cannon said.

Tomahawk glanced up at the lawman.

'Ya sure is a miserable old coot, ain't ya? What ya trying to do? Depress me?'

Cannon laughed. 'I'm sorry, Tomahawk!'

Tomahawk rose up and dusted off his pants with his hands.

'Reckon I'll go and give young Red a hand with the horses, Cannon. Looks like me and Gene are riding home tonight. Darned if I can figure out why.'

Cannon smiled.

'Maybe Gene misses the Bar 10, my friend.'

Tomahawk's eyes wrinkled up as he smiled.

'Yeah, I reckon ya right. I miss the old place as well.'

19

The two horsemen had been riding for hours when they approached the mouth of Devil's Canyon. It was dark and a few thousand stars burned brightly in the large sky above them, competing with the bright moon behind the rider's shoulders. Gene Adams eased back on his reins and plucked one of his canteens off his saddle horn. He unscrewed its stopper and put it to his mouth. The water tasted good.

'Want some?' Adams asked his oldest pal.

Tomahawk nodded and accepted the canteen. He took one mouthful and then returned it to the rancher.

'Ya looks a tad thoughtful, boy.'

'I am, old friend.'

'What ya thinkin' about?' Tomahawk looked at the high-sided canyon ahead of them.

'I'm thinking about everything that happened in the last couple of days, Tomahawk.' Adams took another mouthful of the cool water. 'I'm thinking about Old Man Davis getting himself shot like that. Then us just happening to show up. Reckon our fates are chiselled in marble someplace up yonder. There ain't a lot we can do to change things.'

Tomahawk closed one eye and looked hard at the rider on the tall chestnut mare.

'I'm inclined to agree with ya, Gene. Things sure do seem to happen in a darn weird way and no mistake. I reckon that them fellas would have killed little Nancy if'n we hadn't have tracked them up to the top of the falls.'

Gene Adams then turned around in his saddle and unbuckled one of the straps on his saddle-bags. He took one of the golden coins from the swollen satchel and stared at it in the moonlight. He placed it between his teeth and then smiled.

'I plumb forgot about all that money, Gene!' Tomahawk said as he watched the rancher carefully refasten the small buckle.

'That's why you ain't the Bar 10 treasurer, old-timer.'

'Johnny sure looked happy back there.' Tomahawk sighed. 'I wouldn't be surprised if we don't lose him to that little gal, Gene boy.'

'I don't think we'll lose him just yet. Not whilst there's so many other pretty gals around, Tomahawk,' Adams said wryly. The older rider chuckled.

'He sure is popular, OK.'

Gene Adams screwed the stopper back on his canteen and stared at the canyon. 'We ought to ride hard through the canyon now the sun has set. That'll cut down the time it'll take us to reach the lake by half.'

Tomahawk stroked the neck of his gelding.

'This young horse is fit enough for a good hard ride but what about your old mare there? Is she up to it?'

'She'll outrun your little nag any day of the week, old-timer!'

'Ya wanna make a wager?' Tomahawk's eyes twinkled.

'A silver dollar?'

'Good enough!'

Suddenly both men were distracted by the sound of a galloping rider behind them. They turned and saw Red Hawke thundering towards them on Johnny's pinto pony. He reined in and stopped between their horses.

'I thought you were gonna stay at the hotel with Johnny and Nancy for a week or so?' Adams asked. 'What you doing here, Red boy?'

Red looked even more puzzled than usual. He pushed the brim of his hat off his face and rested his bony elbows on his saddle horn.

'That's what I figured, boss. But after the marshal headed back to McCoy, Johnny and Nancy started to tell me that I ought to be heading home with you.'

Tomahawk winked at the rancher.

'And Johnny let ya borrow his pinto?'

'Sure did!' Red nodded. 'He insisted I take this pony coz it's darn fast.'

'Did Johnny happen to mention when he might be headed back to the Bar 10 himself, Red?' Adams smiled.

'Nope!'

'He'll be back when his lips goes numb!' Tomahawk chuckled.

Adams nodded and lifted his reins.

'C'mon, boys. Let's ride hard and fast. I reckon we'll cover a whole heap of ground before sun-up. I don't want to be still on that desert when the sun rises.'

The three horsemen spurred and thundered across the dusty trail into Devil's Canyon. Their horses ate up the ground beneath their hoofs as they responded to the riders' whooping calls.

Faster and faster the three horses raced straight down the centre of the trail between the towering canyon walls. The sound of their horses' hoofs echoed all around the high canyon.

They had ridden to within a couple

of hundred yards of the end of the treacherous valley when red hot tapers cut through the eerie light from both sides.

Then the sound of outlaw guns and rifles filled their ears as the ground all about them exploded into clouds of dust.

'C'mon, boys!' Adams yelled out. 'Ride like you've never ridden before!'

20

There was nowhere to go. Nowhere to hide. Bullets came from both directions towards the three riders. The outlaws had waited far too long for their quarry to arrive and they were dry and angry. Samson Stone's men did not need him to tell them to fire, they had opened up with venomous fury as soon as the Bar 10 riders were within range.

Then, as the pinto pony rode ahead of the two other horses, Adams and Tomahawk saw their young companion buckle as a bullet hit him. He rolled off his saddle and landed hard.

It was all the two following horsemen could do not to ride over the rolling body of Red.

Adams and Tomahawk dragged at their reins and dropped off the backs of their mounts. The two men ignored the relentless bullets which continued to cut down from both sides and rushed to the fallen cowboy.

'Give me cover!' Adams ordered his pal as he plucked the thin youngster up off the sand and ran to a boulder.

Tomahawk drew his gun and fired as he walked backwards to where Adams stood over Red.

As the old man knelt down beside the unconscious Red, Gene Adams pulled both his golden Colts from their holsters and cocked their hammers.

He started to return fire as more and more bullets got too close for comfort. The rancher moved away from his two men as if trying to draw the fire of their unseen enemies' bullets away from them.

It worked.

Bullets cut away large chunks of a boulder beside the tall rancher. He stopped and fired straight up at the riflemen's own deadly gunsmoke.

He had no idea that his famed accuracy had already cut down Brook Talbot and Poke Green. Then more shots came from above and behind him. Bullets came within inches of him.

Adams swung around and blasted both his legendary golden guns up into the darkness.

A muffled scream came a few seconds before the body of Leroy Chard crashed down the rocks and landed in a bloody heap beside him.

It was a thirsty, desperate Zon Mooney who had moved down the rocks and was headed for the three Bar 10 horses a hundred yards away from the raging battle.

Adams ran from one side of the narrow canyon to the other. A trail of bullets followed his every stride as he hit the rockface and squeezed both his triggers once again.

The rancher gasped and watched as Mooney was hit off his high-heeled cowboy boots by his deadly shots.

Then he felt a torturous pain in his left leg. Adams staggered, then realized that a bullet had gone straight through his calf-muscle just above the top of his high boot. The tall man tried to move and felt himself fall into the dust. The rocks behind him shattered as another half-dozen rifle shots hit it.

Adams holstered one of his smoking Colts and shook the spent shells from the other. He reloaded it and slid it back into its holster. Then, as bullets got closer and closer to him, he untied his bandanna and wrapped it around his leg just below the knee.

He tightened the knot, then drew his loaded gun again.

Adams saw a flash from the canyon wall opposite him. He felt a bullet cut through his shirt-sleeve. He cocked the gun's hammer and fired.

Carson Farmer had showed the rancher too much of a target.

It was his last mistake.

Farmer fell. His lifeless body hit a score of scattered boulders before landing on the canyon floor. Dust rose like a cloud around the body.

For the first time in minutes, the canyon was silent. Adams scrambled back to his feet and cocked the hammer of his gun again. His eyes darted all around the moonlit canyon walls as he slowly made his way towards their horses.

A question burned like a branding-iron into the mind of the wounded rancher as he staggered along the shadowy trail.

Were there any of the bushwhackers left?

If so, how many?

Then Adams caught a fleeting glimpse of a man moving down from high above him. A man with a rifle. The figure was that of Samson Stone. The outlaw leader had realized that he no longer had a gang to obey his orders.

Adams raised his gun and fired. The bullet missed the ruthless outlaw by only a few inches. It was close enough to make Stone turn his Winchester on the injured rancher. The expert hands worked the rifle's mechanism fast and furiously. Bullets cut down into the canyon all around Adams.

He felt the burning heat of the bullets as they passed around him. Dust from the rocks showered over Adams. He could not see a thing.

Then he heard a thud.

Every instinct in the rancher knew that the man had jumped down from the rocks and was now somewhere on the floor of the canyon. Gene Adams felt his heart start to pound inside his chest.

The sound of the outlaw's boots hitting the ground echoed all around him as he stood and moved the gun back and forth searching for a target.

Then a noise caused the rancher to spin on his bleeding leg. A pain carved its way from the bullet-hole to his brain. He staggered again and somehow steadied himself. Adams recognized the distinctive sound of his chestnut mare snorting and whinnying beyond the clouds of stone-dust which had enveloped him.

'Amy!' Adams called out to his horse.

Suddenly a rifle shot deafened him.

He just caught sight of a blinding red taper as the bullet came straight at his face. He raised his golden Colt and was knocked off his feet as the bullet hit the side of his gun.

Adams hit the ground and saw the legs of Samson Stone.

They were walking towards him. He could also see the lowered rifle barrel with smoke trailing from it.

'Is that you, Adams?' Stone shouted out. 'Did I kill ya or are ya still lucky?'

'I'm still lucky!' Adams muttered to himself. Without even thinking, Adams swiftly raised his .45 and tried to fire it, but the gun was damaged. He dropped it at his side, dragged the other weapon from its holster and squeezed its trigger. This gun would not respond either. Feverishly, Adams opened the weapon and shook the spent bullet-casings from its hot chamber.

His fingers searched for bullets along the front of his gunbelt. Racing against time, Adams pushed each of them into the holes and then closed the rotating chamber back into the body of the Colt.

Then he saw Stone's boots again.

They were now only twenty feet away.

The dust began to clear and both men stared into each other's eyes through the blue moonlit canyon.

Their weapons were aimed straight at one another.

'Who are you?' Adams asked.

'Samson Stone!'

'Never heard of you.'

Stone frowned. His eyes burned the air between them.

'I'm the man who stole all ya gold, Adams!'

'Not yet you ain't!' Adams said.

Then a rumbling sound washed over both men. It grew louder and louder with every heartbeat. Something was coming. And it was coming their way. It sounded like a freight train, but both men knew that there were no tracks anywhere near Devil's Canyon.

Neither man was willing to turn his

head away and take his eyes from those of his adversary.

'What is that?' Stone's voice sounded alarmed.

'Riders!' Adams said knowingly. 'A whole heap of riders by the sounds of it, Stone!'

Samson Stone took a step backwards, yet kept his rifle aimed at the rancher on the ground before him.

'Where you going?' Adams asked.

'Reckon I'll just take ya horse and the gold, Adams!' Stone replied as he reached the three horses. His left hand searched the air for the chestnut mare's reins. Then he found them.

Gene Adams raised his golden gun and trained it at the outlaw's head.

'I wouldn't do that if I was you!' he warned.

'You ain't me!' Stone squeezed his trigger.

The magazine of the Winchester was empty.

Adams eased his index finger back. The gun fired. He watched as Samson

Stone was lifted off the ground and then crashed down between the horses.

Then he looked to where the sound was coming from. He saw Rip Calloway leading the rest of the Bar 10 riders towards the canyon.

Adams holstered his guns and clawed his way up the rocks until he was standing. He rested a gloved hand on the rockface and looked across at Tomahawk and Red.

The old-timer was sitting with his bearded face buried in his hands beside the motionless young cowboy.

Gene Adams lowered his head. He feared the worst.

Finale

Clouds of dust rose up into the air off the hoofs of the Bar 10 riders' mounts. Before it had time to settle, Rip and Happy and most of the other cowboys had dismounted and gathered all around their wounded leader. Happy moved close to the rancher and allowed Adams to rest his weight on his sturdy shoulders.

'What happened here, Gene?' Rip asked as the cowboys grabbed the reins of the three horses.

'Bushwhacked!' Adams said bluntly. He continued to stare at the weeping Tomahawk. 'Some critters thought they'd get rich the easy way.'

'Who are they?'

Adams shrugged and pointed at the body of Stone.

'That was called Samson Stone!' He sighed. 'He's the critter that we kept bumping into back at McCoy! I knew he was too damned interested in us.'

'How many were there, Gene?' Larry Drake asked as the cowboys gathered all around the rancher.

'Too many!' Adams answered.

'You kill them all?' Rip wondered.

Gene Adams's eyes darted all around the rocks.

'I sure hope so.'

Rip turned and stared across at Tomahawk.

'Who's that lying next to Tomahawk, Gene?'

'It must be Johnny!' Happy gasped as he helped Adams towards the old-timer. 'That's his pinto back there, ain't it?'

'It ain't Johnny, Happy,' Adams corrected.

'Then who is it?' Rip questioned as all the Bar 10 cowboys moved behind the limping rancher towards the sobbing Tomahawk.

'Red!' Adams replied quietly.

The cowboys suddenly went quiet.

Gene Adams nodded to Happy and

then moved away from the rotund cowboy. He limped up to the rockface and eased himself down on the sand between Tomahawk and Red.

He rested a gloved hand on the bony shoulder of the weeping old man and then squeezed it.

'Take it easy, Tomahawk. You could drown folks.'

Tomahawk pulled his face from his hands and looked around at the stunned, silent cowboys. Even the moonlight could not disguise the fact that his eyes were bloodshot. Tears rolled down his wrinkled face and disappeared into his beard.

'Gee, it's good to see ya all,' he mumbled.

Adams patted the old-timer's back, then looked at Red. The youngster did not move.

'He was a good kid!'

Tomahawk nodded.

'In all the years we've been raising cattle, he's the only one who liked my cookin'.'

Adams placed a hand on Red's shoulder and leaned over the body. He carefully turned him over and stared at the awkward face of the young cowboy. Adams looked at Tomahawk and then at the rest of the cowboys. There was a curious expression on his face as he leaned closer to Red.

Adams started to slap the cheeks of the motionless figure.

Tomahawk gasped.

'What ya doin', Gene boy? Stop hittin' him. Ain't ya got no respect for the dead?'

Adams continued to slap the cowboy.

'He ain't dead, you old fool!'

Tomahawk jumped on to his bony knees.

'He ain't?'

Red's eyes fluttered and then slowly opened. He looked all around him and smiled at the two closest faces.

'What happened, boss?'

'You was shot, Red boy!' Tomahawk nodded briskly.

Gene Adams smiled.

'You was also nearly buried by this old fossil, Red.'

'Huh?' Red gulped.

'Ya should have ducked, son!' Tomahawk grinned.

Adams looked at his Bar 10 cowboys and smiled.

'Come on, boys. It's a long ride to the Bar 10!'

THE END

Other titles in the
Linford Western Library:

KILLINGS AT LETANA CREEK

Bill Williams

Retired United States marshal Ned Thomas rides to Letana Creek to help a friend who fears being the next victim of a serial killer. But Ned makes matters worse for his friend's family and puts his own life in danger. Ned will need all his guile to solve the mystery surrounding the killings and to confront the Molloy brothers, unexpectedly released from prison. They are hell-bent on revenge. But those who write him off as a has-been are sorely mistaken . . .

McBRIDE RIDES OUT

John Dyson

It all began when the Buckthorn Kid smashed his way out of jail. Before long there was a $40,000 hold-up on the railroad, and then murder and mayhem in Medora . . . Montana rancher Randolph McBride is on the trail of stolen cattle when he discovers the rustlers have joined forces with the train robbers . . . Now the lead really begins to fly and McBride's life is on the line. Will his fight for justice succeed?

THE MANHUNTERS

Dean Edwards

Young cowboy Clu Marvin finishes a cattle drive in McCoy and sets about enjoying his pay with some pals. But Sheriff Dan Brown has spotted Marvin's resemblance to the outlaw the Reno Kid ... Soon, Brown and his corrupt boss, Lex Reason, plan to snatch Marvin and use him to claim the reward for the Reno Kid. Desperately, Marvin attempts to escape from the deadly duo. What follows is a bloodbath, leaving Marvin riding for his life — hotly pursued by the manhunters ...

RUSTLER ROUNDUP

George J. Prescott

Cord Wheeler, the El Paso detective, is a bodyguard to cattle dealer Jase Elford, for a journey down to Santiago. But, at their destination, Elford is murdered and Wheeler is caught up in a rustling scam. Amidst the corruption, an innocent boy is due to be hanged for Elford's killing. Wheeler's task of stopping the rustlers means finding their secret hideout . . . In a running fight across the badlands, Wheeler must take on the gang and win if justice is to be served.